Falling
FROM
GRAVITY

USA TODAY BESTSELLING AUTHOR

K.K. ALLEN

Cover design by Sarah Hansen | Okay Creations
Cover photography by Perrywinkle Photography
Edited by Red Adept Editing
Book design by Inkstain Design Studio

For more information, please write to SayHello@KK-Allen.com

ISBN: 978-1-07-600862-6

Falling FROM GRAVITY

Dear Reader,

In an effort to give you an interactive experience, YouTube links have been included throughout this book with no copyright infringement intended. All links point to their rightful owners, and all owners have been contacted regarding the use of video in this publication. Viewing the videos is not required to read, however, my intention is to bring you the inspiration that went into creating this story while you follow along.

Enjoy!

K.K.

Chapter 1

AMELIA

A loud hiss shot through the air as I exited my car and stepped onto the shoulder of Latigo Canyon Road. I groaned as my eyes made contact with the damage. I wasn't even five minutes away from my home when my silver Miata found its way into a pothole. *Just my luck.*

I crouched slowly, staring at the deflating tire as a slew of curse words flew through my mind. I scolded the punctured rubber with a shake of my head. "You had one job."

I had approximately an hour and a half to get to Los Angeles, and with traffic, I was already cutting it close.

Looking around, I debated who I could call to get me out of this mess. My parents would call for a tow then a car service to drive me straight home, where I was certain to get a lecture about being aware of my surroundings. Or I could contact my best friend and neighbor, Trinity, who I knew was in the middle of studying for her big chemistry exam.

As much as I hated myself for choosing to interrupt Trinity, it was my only true option. Her response was instant.

Trin: *Help is on its way!*

My next breath was a deep one, whooshing out of me along with the tension I'd felt moments earlier. Trinity was the kind of friend who didn't hesitate to help her bestie out in a jam, no matter what was going on in her life. I would buy her Starbucks and convince her to drive me to LA. She could study there.

Ugh. My gut twisted at my selfish thoughts, but I couldn't stay another day in Malibu. Everything I loved was in LA. Well, besides Trinity. She was the only reason I stuck around as much as I did. But with us both graduating in a few months, I couldn't hang back while she studied to pursue her dreams. I had my own dreams to fulfill. Big dreams. And they all started with Gravity Dance Complex.

Stuffing my disappointment deep into my chest, I crawled into the passenger seat of my car, turned up the volume of Katy Perry's "Wide Awake," and slouched in my seat, propping my heel on the open door.

Not even a minute later, I started at the familiar sound of an approaching engine. *No.* My eyes widened, my cheeks burned red, and my chest immediately filled with panic. *She wouldn't.* That wasn't the sound of just any engine, and one glance through my windshield confirmed my suspicion.

The newly restored white 1966 Chevrolet C/K was practically a celebrity in our town, always causing a stir wherever it appeared. And it was owned by none other than Tobias James—otherwise known as Trinity's brother and Malibu's quintessential heartthrob.

"Malibu Gold" was what the locals called him: a star in the making. He was known best for his high school basketball shooting record, but that wasn't the only thing we all found impressive. He'd also maintained a perfect GPA throughout school.

Athletic, smart, and good-looking—*that* was Malibu Gold. Beyond the white sandy beaches and being home to a Pepperdine University campus, Malibu had Tobias to give the locals bragging rights.

At least that had been the case until he'd bailed halfway through his first season of playing college basketball for the Pepperdine Waves with no explanations or apologies. He'd simply dropped out of school before winter quarter and *stayed* gone for months. No one could find him, and the police wouldn't do anything since he was no longer a minor.

When he'd finally returned a few months later, he didn't try to go back to school, and the Waves had already ended their basketball season with a losing record, which—of course—they blamed on Tobias. He was the obvious easy target since he hadn't even tried to defend himself, but it was still wrong. All of it.

The once social butterfly was now a recluse, a drifter who came in and out of town as he pleased, picking up odd jobs at the local body shop or working on his truck. He was stoic, quiet, and disgruntled. The drastic change made me wonder how much of what Trinity had told me was true. She'd said her brother's behavior was all for nothing. Or maybe there was something she was hiding. My gut, and Trinity's inability to look me in the eyes, told me it was the latter.

Trinity had mentioned he was in town again, not that she'd had to tell me with the way gossip in our neighborhood worked, but I didn't understand why she would send *him* to rescue me. Tobias and I had barely spoken a word to each other since elementary school. Not only that, but every time I was around him, my senses jumbled into a big, tangled ball, triggering every inch of awkwardness I owned.

He slammed the door of his truck, snapping me to attention as his long strides brought him to me. The slight angle to his jaw appeared hard as a rock, and there was a deep crease between his brows as he eyed the tire that had failed me.

"What happened here?" he grumbled. My imagination was strong, but the utter annoyance in his tone was one-hundred-percent real.

"Pothole." I stepped out of the car and stood near him, folding my arms across my chest. "Shredded my damn tire."

His frown deepened before he knelt to inspect the damage. "Shredded would be the correct word." He wiped his hands on his jeans and stood up. "Got a spare?"

I pointed at the trunk. "Be my guest."

I watched him work in silence since I assumed that was how he would want it. While he did, I looked at him up close for what felt like the first time. His dark hair curled just below his ear lobes, and his wide shoulders stretched the white fabric across his back. His legs were so thick, I could see that even through his jeans, they carried a definition that could only be built by an athlete.

I'd gotten good at pretending he wasn't around when he very much was, because avoidance was better than the repercussions would be. Trinity would never approve of my attraction to her brother. She'd said as much when we were fourteen and mock-cheerleading a basketball game in our neighborhood park.

"You can't date my brother, you know?" Trinity had said, her eyes narrowed on me as I executed a perfect toe touch.

I faltered slightly on my landing before doing a double take. Her stare was so accusing, like she knew about the crush I'd always had on her brother.

"That would just be weird." She let out a breathy laugh before rolling her eyes. "And we could never be friends again."

Why she'd decided to speak up in that moment was beyond me. Had I been staring? Probably. But it was her idea to show up in those damn miniskirts.

When she jumped back into the cheer, like she hadn't just crushed my soul, I'd made my decision to let whatever feelings that had been festering for Tobias go. My friendship with Trinity was too important, and I would never let a boy come between us.

When he spoke again, my eyes jumped in his direction, locking on his grayish-blue ones. They appeared almost silver with the way the sunlight hit them, matching the key that dangled from a chain he wore around his neck. I was so busy staring, I completely missed what he'd said.

"Do you have far to go?" he repeated, irritation seeping into his tone.

"Um." *Where am I headed again?* "Yeah. LA, actually." My eyes caught on his grease-stained hands. "Thanks for taking care of this. I might actually make it in time." I stepped around him and toward the front of my car, relief filling me in a rush.

"Whoa." His arm shot out, blocking my path. "You can't drive to LA on that tire. You need to get it replaced with a real one."

My face fell, and I groaned, crossing my arms to hug myself as the weight of disappointment crushed my chest. I'd only waited my entire life for this audition. If I didn't get to LA that day, my dreams were over. I couldn't let that happen. This was my chance, and I could feel it so deeply, it reached my bones. My entire body ached at the vision of what waited for me by the end of the day. I just had to get there.

When I peered up at him again, a thought struck me. "Can you take me?"

His gaze snapped to mine so hard, I wouldn't have been surprised if it triggered whiplash. "Take you where?"

"To LA."

His chest rose, and lines began to gather on his forehead. "That's an hour away, Amelia."

"An hour and a half with traffic," I corrected. *Probably not the best move on my part.*

He blew out a breath and shook his head. "Look, I promised Trinity I'd help you get home. She said nothing about driving your ass to LA. Don't your parents have a driver or something?" He shook his head and shoved his fingers through his hair. "I'm sure you'll figure it out."

Panic quickly replaced the relief I had felt only seconds before. There was no way I could trust one of my parents' staff to take me to LA without it starting up the dreaded conversation about my future.

Ideas clicked through my mind until one fell from my mouth. "I could buy you dinner after."

The look Tobias gave me was tortured with disbelief. "What makes you think I'd want to go to dinner with you?"

I swallowed my embarrassment then scrunched my face in frustration. He was right. There was no enticement in forcing him to eat dinner with me on top of it all. But I was getting desperate.

"Then how about an I-O-U? If you ever need anything from me, just say the word." He didn't fight back immediately, so I widened my eyes, letting him know I was serious. "Anything."

He let out a frustrated growl, and that was when I knew I had him.

I jumped in again. "Look, I know it's an inconvenience, but I wouldn't ask if it wasn't important. I *need* to get to LA. Will you please help me get there?"

He looked away then raised his hands over his head in surrender. "Fine. But you're going to owe me. *Big*." He enunciated the last word as he hovered over me, most likely trying to intimidate me. That wasn't hard considering his body doubled mine in size. "And you can't tell Trin about this. She'll murder me if she finds out we went to LA without her."

I squealed and jumped in my spot. "Deal."

He was right about Trinity murdering someone, but I knew that someone wouldn't be him.

Chapter 2

AMELIA

I'd never been so nervous in my life, not even the time I auditioned for a leading role in our community theater's performance of *Moving Out*—which I nailed, by the way. But knowing I would be riding in Tobias's truck, alone with him and his questionable temperament, I had no clue what I'd gotten myself into.

Luckily, he turned up the volume on some Nirvana song as soon as I hopped in. I took it as a silent warning to not give him a reason to turn it down. And like a good girl, I sat there, buckled tight, eyes glued out my window, and sweaty palms pressed against my black leggings.

His deep rasp broke the silence thirty minutes later. "You been thinking about college?"

I swallowed back my shock at hearing his voice before repeating his question in my head.

"No," I said, turning toward him. "No college for me." I timidly watched him, sure judgment would follow my answer as it always did with my parents. They believed in my dreams, but they wanted what most parents wanted for their children—for them to get a degree to fall back on *when*, not if, their dreams failed.

I didn't need a fallback plan. I had dance, and dance was it for me.

But his expression didn't fill with judgment. He exhibited a patience that was actually comforting.

My pulse sped when I caught his eyes flick from my lips to my attire.

"What kind of dance do you, uh, *do* again?"

Of course he had to ask. I didn't expect him to remember the talent show he'd attended with his sister last year. In it, I had dressed up like Britney—in the full "I'm A Slave 4 U" ensemble, complete with a yellow plastic snake wrapped around my neck—and lip-synced my way to my first-place trophy.

"Everything," I said. "But mostly contemporary jazz and hip-hop. I dance at this studio in LA…" I blushed, catching myself and cringing at my need to overshare. When it came to my passion, it was hard not to.

Tobias's nose flared. "Please don't tell me I'm taking you to a dance class right now."

Everything inside me heated with embarrassment. I turned toward the passenger window, folding my arms across my chest. "It's important. I don't expect *you* to understand."

"What the hell does that mean?"

I shook my head while my jaw clenched so tightly, my cheeks burned. My thoughts were unkind. It wasn't fair for me to compare his dreams to mine. I couldn't begin to assume what would make him throw everything away like he had.

"I bailed on my plans to take your ass to LA. You owe me an explanation. Why am I taking you to a *dance* class on a Saturday? Why now? Why today?"

I suppressed the scream of frustration building in the back of my throat. "It's not a dance class. It's an audition for an NBA halftime performance. I can't just go another time. The Lions Dance Squad only has one performance like this a year."

"The Lions?" He threw me an incredulous look. "You're auditioning for the LA Lions Dance Team? The season's almost over." He stated it like he was informing me of something I didn't already know. Then he laughed condescendingly. "Never mind that. Aren't you a little young to be dancing for them anyway? News flash. You're still in high school, kid."

My eyes blazed, and I could feel the blood boiling in my chest. "I'm old enough," I said through gritted teeth. "It's just a halftime performance. If I can secure a spot for this, then I become an instant finalist in team auditions this summer. I need to make that team."

He had no idea how big this dream was or how easily I could visualize myself on that court with a squad full of talented dancers in front of a pumped-up crowd.

Silence descended upon us for the next few minutes, and I didn't dare glance his way again. He was either amused by my dreams or pissed off by them. I didn't want to acknowledge either.

"Why LA?" he finally spat out. "Why the Lions? There are teams all over the country."

My shoulders lifted with my breath, and I let it out in a sigh before turning back to him. "I don't know. My dad loves the Lions. I love the Lions. And I've always pictured my dance career starting and ending in LA." I shrugged. "It's as simple as that."

"It's as simple as that, huh?" He asked the question like it made him angry. "Dreams never come true that easily, Amelia. It takes time, effort."

I focused on him with stern eyes, enraged that he would dare test my passion or the reality of my dreams. "I know, *Tobias*," I said, making sure to enunciate his name with as much flair as he'd spoken mine. "I've been training at Gravity since I was a kid. I know my odds in the world of professional dance, and they're good."

"Gravity?"

"Gravity Dance Complex. It's a huge dance center, and I don't just mean in size. Well, it's that too. But Gravity is affiliated with the A-Listers of Hollywood. Producers, casting agents, singers, actors, stage directors, cruise ship entertainment—you name it."

"So you're telling me with all that opportunity at your fingertips, *your* dream is to dance professionally for the NBA?"

I nodded. "Yes. To start." My eyes curiously flickered over his profile. I wanted to ask him what had happened to *his* dreams. We'd always had basketball in common. And while we'd never been close, just that simple dream had made me feel like we were connected in some strange way.

"I just want to dance. And making a living is a necessity since I don't plan to get help from my parents. I need to do this on my own so I don't feel like I owe them anything."

"Let me guess—they want you to take over the family business."

My parents owned a production company in Malibu, which had grown to be pretty successful. They'd expanded since the beginning, investing in a plethora of sports and entertainment franchises. My father loved to have his hands in all the pies, and my mom supported that, but her focus was on their original investment at Quinten Clark Entertainment.

My laughter came hard at Tobias's comment. "Are you kidding? My dad would never loosen the reins on his baby." I shook my head. "No. Quinten Clark will never give up control. But work for him?" I nodded. "Absolutely. He always thought I'd make a great face for his company."

"That sounds horrible."

I shrugged. "It's not as awful as it sounds. His parents were in the business too. He's always been a family-company type of man. I promised him I'd still try to make it to the big parties, but that was the best I could do." I flashed him a smile to help relieve some of the tension that had grown between us.

It seemed to work, though silence fell again and lasted until we were a mile away from the off-ramp.

"The exit is up ahead," I warned. After guiding him to the front curb of the tall brick building that had become my second home, I got out and held the door open to speak to him. "You don't have to wait. I can find a ride home."

His eyes narrowed. "I'm taking you home, Amelia. When should I be back?"

"Um…" My eyes floated to the dash, where I read the time. "It's hard to say. If I make it all the way through, I could be here until ten tonight."

He nodded, signaling for me to shut the door. "I'll be back at ten, then."

Is there any use arguing with him?

With a subtle sigh, I gripped the door. "Ten o'clock it is. Thanks, Tobias."

He didn't respond, so I shut the door. As he drove off, I couldn't help but wonder where he would go… and if he really would come back.

Chapter 3

AMELIA

In my rush from the registration desk to the main dance studio, I felt my very first heartbreak.

"Amie, wait up."

Janelle, one of the choreographers of Gravity was jogging toward me with my headshot in her hands. My heart sank instantly. I didn't know why she was about to turn me away, but I knew by the apology written into her expression and her sorrowful eyes that I'd made Tobias drive me to LA for no reason.

"Everything okay?" I asked, unable to shake the nerves from my voice.

Her head tilt and sigh knotted my insides. "I'm so sorry, Amie. I know how badly you want this. And you're more than talented enough to make it..."

"But?"

Janelle nodded. "*But* you're only seventeen. I can't even let you into that audition room."

My jaw fell. I knew there was a possibility I could get turned away, but I didn't think my age would be the deciding factor. *I can fix this.*

"No, it's okay." I scrambled to pull my ID from my phone case and handed it to her. "See?" My eyes lit, and relief started to spread through me. "I'll be eighteen next week."

Janelle frowned and shook her head. "I'm just the messenger here, Amie. If it were up to me, you know I'd let you audition. But according to the NBA, you have to be eighteen by the time of this audition today. I am so sorry."

Her eyes lit up, and I knew she was going to try to cushion the blow. It was what she was good at in situations like these. Rejection was not an easy pill to swallow, and Janelle was often the bearer of bad news. Being a professional choreographer in the industry, she had to be.

"That doesn't mean you can't still try out for the team this summer," she said. "I'll even write you a recommendation you can attach to your resumé. I've worked with the team before, and you're good, Amie. You'll stand out on your own."

Her encouragement should have lit up my insides like the Fourth of July, but I was too stuck in the moment of rejection. I'd had a plan. And that plan had an end result that was threatened because of bad timing.

Long after Janelle left me standing in a puddle of my misery, I fled the audition space, found the first dance studio, and slipped inside. The class was in mid-choreography, but no one stopped me from taking a spot on the floor and joining in. I didn't know what else to do for the next eight hours before Tobias got there. I couldn't call him to pick me up. That would require calling Trinity to get his number and having to explain why he'd taken me to LA in the first place. I'd rather drown in a puddle of my disappointment.

Besides, dance had always been my therapy. One shattered dream wouldn't change that, and I needed dance now more than ever. Quite simply, I could get lost in dance. So I did.

I hopped from one class to the next, learning choreography from all styles of dance. I threw every ounce of frustration and passion into each routine, splattering it all on the gloss-stained wood floors.

"Damn, girl, you are on fire tonight," said Arnie, another dancer who was entering class behind me. It would be ten o'clock by the time this one ended, but I was still riding on whatever adrenaline rush I'd caught earlier in the day.

Before I could respond, my eyes caught on my friend Lance, who was nuzzling noses with Vivian Gray, the choreographer for Hot Heels, my last class of the night.

When did that happen? I hated how much I missed not living in LA. It was like a completely different world, one in which I belonged more than I ever felt like I did in Malibu.

The lovebirds were still crowding the door when I slipped past them and found a group of familiar faces. It looked like several regulars, or Lifers as we called each other, were taking this class. I pulled my bag from my shoulder and sat beside Arnie, who was focused on the way his shaved calves looked when they glowed under the studio light. I laughed, catching his attention.

He shot me an amused glare. "Don't stare too hard, girl, or those big eyes might just go falling out of that skinny head of yours."

"I wasn't staring." I pulled my shoes out of my bag with a grin. "Just admiring. You get a cleaner shave than I ever could."

He barked out a laugh. "Shave? Oh, hell no. I lasered that shit off last year. Best investment of my life." He stood then popped his hip in my direction before strutting toward the front of the room.

"Ohhh, let me see those." Another dancer, Mandy, plopped down beside me. Her eyes were huge on my knee-length, heeled denim boots. "I need these." She ran her hand up and down the material, inspecting every seam, every manufactured tear, and every angle. "Where did you get them?"

"Some Etsy store. I'll send you the link tonight. Hey"—I nodded to the door—"when did Lance and Viv start up?"

Mandy flipped her braids over her shoulder as she sneaked a glance at them. She immediately turned back in my direction and made a gagging face. "It's recent. We were at Carter's a few nights ago, and it just happened. One second, they were laughing together like normal, and then the next second, they were dry humping on the couch for all to see."

"No way." I laughed with disbelief. Surely, she was exaggerating.

Mandy shrugged. "You should have been there to witness it yourself. It was soft-porn action, and we didn't even have to subscribe."

I laughed. "Okay, okay. Enough about Lance and Viv. Why didn't I get an invite to this red-room party?"

"Like you would have come," she replied with a scoff. "You say no whenever you're not already in town."

"Do you blame me? The drive is painful as it is. I can't do that twice in one day."

Mandy's eyes twinkled. "Not long until you'll be in LA. Then you won't have to worry about that stupid commute."

Ugh. She was right. I couldn't wait for the day I lived closer to Gravity. I'd been counting down since last summer.

"Strap up, you sexy beasts," Viv called as she leapt across the dance floor. "It's time for a showdown if you know what I mean." She wiggled her eyebrows at us, but I didn't know what she meant until the music started a few seconds later and Britney's song "Showdown" blasted through the loudspeakers.

I could feel the energy of the class spike instantly. There was something about the pop diva's tunes that hyped a dancer. I forgot everything except for the beat that pumped from deep inside me. I felt like I was in a dark room alone with the music.

Viv started with a slow cat walk on the first eight counts, followed by a few sexy counts to bring us to our knees for the start of floor work. Usually when I took a heels class, I assumed we would be on our knees a lot. At first, it had been painful, but I'd learned quickly how to balance my weight in the right positions to avoid the strain that could mess my body up.

It always blew my mind when anyone challenged the fact that dancers were athletes. I couldn't think of another profession that combined more muscles, more brain power, and more energy than dance.

We'd completed the dance and had run it a few times from top to bottom when Viv stopped the music and shouted, "Performance time."

The room broke into a collective cheer. That was what we looked forward to in every class—a chance to take everything we'd learned and go all out, putting our own flair into someone else's creation. It didn't matter if someone was an introvert outside the studio; when he or she walked onto the dance floor, they were transformed. And Viv was an incredible creator.

Viv searched the room, examining each of us. "Let me have…" She tapped her chin one more time. "Mandy…" Mandy shot forward with a squeal. "Dustin…" His buddy clapped him on the shoulder before he took off to join Mandy. "And…" Her eyes connected with my hopeful ones. "And Amie."

I kind of loved that they called me Amie at Gravity when no one did back home. It felt like I was a completely different person among my peers, with whom I shared a mutual passion.

Viv clapped her hands. "Pick your groups, and then let's do this, yeah?" She knew the three of us well enough to know we understood the drill. She'd just chosen us to lead each dance, which meant we were allowed to pick backup dancers to join us for our performances.

Even though my focus in the mirror had been on myself, I'd caught sight of a few dancers that had impressed me. I went to them first and asked them to join me, and it was as simple as that. I had my team.

But when I turned around to face the first group, led by Viv, I noticed the crowd beginning to gather outside the room. Lance was there too, staring in with a grin on his face as Viv began to move. He watched her like she was the only female on earth, like he couldn't believe he hadn't seen her sooner. It created an ache in me I could only define as envy. I wanted that. I wanted someone who I made sense with, someone who shared my same dream, someone who understood me like no one else.

I'd always told myself I would end up with a dancer, someone who could understand the grueling schedules and the unbridled passion for the arts. Sure, it could be difficult when we left for a gig, but jobs didn't last forever. And I was certain, beyond a shadow of a doubt, I would meet that someone at Gravity.

"You're up, Amie," Viv called.

I winked at my group and nodded to the floor. "Let's do this."

WATCH: SHOW DOWN
smarturl.it/Defying_ShowDown

We were in the last two eight-counts of floor work during the freestyle at the end of the dance when I made the mistake of glancing back at the window. I didn't know why I did it. I wasn't searching for Tobias, but a feeling in my gut told me to look anyway.

The moment my eyes crashed into his, something else awoke inside me, something I'd never felt, even on the dance floor. My head spun, and my heart whirred wildly in my chest. And for a second, I forgot that I was executing a sexy combination, one in which I was wearing nothing but knee-high boots, an oversized cream sweater dress, and black spanks.

I saw him. And deep down, I knew for the first time ever that he saw me too.

Chapter 4

TOBIAS

I'd known Amelia a decade before I truly saw her. I wasn't blind to her good looks, but there was something about hearing her talk about her love of dance that sparked a fire in me.

I began to crave her, and not in a creepy stare-at-her-through-her-bedroom-window sort of way. I wanted her in a way that fueled the spark she'd already lit within me. I wanted to hear her laugh, watch her smile, and catch her fruity scent as she breezed down the hall past my room. It was all bait that lured me in to what I ultimately had to have. Her. In every sense of the word. Because Amelia Clark was the girl who gave me a reason to stay.

And that was exactly why one week after driving her to and from LA, I packed my things and planned to get the hell out of town as soon as possible.

"You haven't disappeared yet."

I was buried under my truck in the middle of an oil change when I heard her stroll into my garage. Her voice was muffled, but I would've known that sweet song anywhere. It was her.

After adjusting the oil pan, I rolled out from under my truck to find Amelia standing there in one of her midriff-baring dance outfits, her hands on her hips. A smile lit up her face, but her eyes were what held me.

I'd always considered my truck and I alike in many ways. Once upon a time, I was the talk of the town—star athlete, catching eyes wherever I went. My dreams had been in the palm of my hand. The fire inside me had been fierce and unstoppable. But after all the bullshit went down, I neglected myself. I sat too long, and eventually, all the parts that had fueled me gave out. No matter how many times or how hard I tried to repair it, there was no going back to original condition.

Is that how she sees me too? Broken and no good? And why do I care?

I continued to stare at her as she moved from the entrance of the garage to the red toolbox on my right. She looked so innocent and curious among my mess of vehicle parts, like she knew she didn't belong, yet there was nowhere else she would rather be.

"How do you know how all this stuff works?"

It was then that I realized I hadn't spoken a word since she'd arrived. "My dad taught me. We used to spend a lot of time in here before..."

"Before what?" She was so nonchalant as she asked, I wondered if Trinity had told her anything. They had been best friends forever, but Trinity had a sort of lioness pride that she risked for no one, just like our parents. Trinity's image was far too important to her, especially when it came to Amelia. Those two were stark opposites, and from the way Trinity spoke about her, I got the impression my sister harbored a deep jealousy.

"Just... before." I wasn't in the mood to set up a conflict between those two.

Amelia nodded, signaling that she wasn't going to push it, as she continued to inspect every gadget and surface with a graze of her finger.

Her eyes drifted to mine as I stood. "Are you leaving again soon?"

"Is that any of your business?" I should have felt bad when her cheeks turned pink from my question, but I felt something else instead—a desire I hadn't felt in a long time.

"Guess not," she said with a roll of her eyes.

I hadn't meant to come off so abrupt. It had just been a long time since I'd flirted with anyone.

Is that what I'm doing? Flirting with my sister's best friend? Because it feels like I'm being a complete jackass.

I leaned against my truck and folded my arms. "Trin left for New York with our parents for spring break."

Amelia nodded as she averted her eyes. They were glued to a hammer drill when she spoke. "Yeah, I know."

"You don't usually stop by when she isn't around."

She gazed up with a shrug. "Guess I was just curious."

"About the type of oil I use on my truck?"

She glared at me. "No, smart-ass." She gestured to the oil dripping into the pan beneath my truck. "I saw you working on her and thought maybe you were leaving again. And..."

My curiosity peaked. "Spit it out, Amelia."

She was chewing nervously on her bottom lip. "I thought maybe I could come with you."

"No." My response was instant. I didn't even have to think twice about it. "There's no fucking way. Your parents would freak. My sister would kill me. And I'm pretty sure the cops would have every reason to arrest me for kidnapping an underage girl without her parents' permission."

"My parents are out of town. Trinity doesn't even have to know about it. And *I'm* pretty sure turning eighteen today puts me in the legal range to do what I want."

My heartbeat sped. "It's your birthday?"

She nodded, and it was then that I saw something else in her eyes—a sadness she'd masked with her smile and her sexy strut up my drive.

Shit.

"So, can we go?" she asked again, her eyes bright and hopeful.

I let out a sigh, hating my instinct to give the girl whatever she wanted. Amelia Clark made me weak, and I couldn't succumb to her power.

"I travel alone."

"Why?"

I grew anxious at her insistence and at my desire to give in so quickly. I wasn't in my right mind. That was the only explanation. It didn't matter if Amelia was of legal age to do whatever she damn well pleased. She couldn't do those things with me.

"I don't know. To get away from people. To think."

She took a step closer to me. "We don't have to talk."

I narrowed my eyes, silently calling her bluff. "You'll be bored out of your mind."

"I won't," she argued.

"There aren't any cell phones where I'm going."

"I wasn't planning to bring mine with me."

"You won't even last one week out there."

"Try me."

Stubborn, stubborn girl. Maybe if she knows where I'm going, she'll drop it.

"How do you feel about camping? And I'm not talking about a cottage in the woods, Amelia. I'm talking about a tent in the middle of nowhere."

She shrugged, clearly determined to agree to any condition I laid out. "I've never done it before." Then she tilted her head. "Sounds like fun."

I chuckled. "Fun is not what I would call it. There aren't any showers on site, so we'd have to drive to get to one. It gets cold at night, hot during the day, and there's no thermostat if you want to get comfortable."

"Where would we sleep?"

"I set up a tent in my truck bed. There's a mattress, but there's only one." I figured that alone would turn her off from hopping in my truck. Accommodations were limited, and she would have to sleep next to me.

"What will we do during the day?"

I shrugged. "Whatever you want to do, Amelia." My eyes flickered over her attire again. Something about the way she eyed me back with that challenging spark made my dick so hard, which was yet another reason why she should back the hell away and forget she'd ever asked me.

Her eyes lit up, sensing my resolve crumbling. "So I can come?"

I turned away from her, placing the wrench back on the wall and strutting back to my truck. "Guess we'll find out," I mumbled to myself. Then I spoke loud enough for her to hear me. "I'll swing by your place in three hours. Be ready to leave."

When I glanced at her over my shoulder, I halted at her smile. Just the fact that I'd put it there made my heart whirl in my chest. And in that single moment I feared that I would also be the one who made it fade.

Chapter 5

AMELIA

He'd warned me, but I was too hurt and stubborn to care where I would spend that week. I just knew I didn't want to be alone. Everyone had forgotten my birthday—my parents, my best friend, my extended family at Gravity. It was like I didn't even exist on my special day. Gravity closing down for that entire week was icing on the cake.

It wasn't like me to dwell in my own misery. I had always been admired for staying positive in any situation. So when I drove up my drive and saw Tobias's long legs sticking out from under his truck, the idea to invite myself wherever he was going was glaringly bright. I figured he must have been planning to leave if he was working on his truck.

"Be ready in three hours," he'd told me before we parted.

I knew the last thing he wanted was a tagalong. But I was excited nonetheless.

It was ten minutes after one o'clock in the afternoon when he turned the corner and I could see his white, antique truck driving toward me. After he parked, he hopped out and took the two suitcases standing at my feet. He didn't even make a wisecrack about the amount of luggage I carried. He just took them, one in each hand, and laid them in the bed of his truck.

"Ready?" he asked when my bags were loaded.

I swallowed and nodded, suddenly feeling a wild flock of flutters in my chest. I'd half expected to never see him again after he'd agreed to let me join him. Surely, the thought crossed his mind to leave without me.

"Hop in." He pulled open the passenger door and waited until my legs were tucked inside before closing it behind me. As he did, our eyes met through the glass. It was a brief moment, but all our intentions were as transparent as air. There was something more neither of us wanted to say aloud.

It wasn't until we'd pulled onto the main highway that I turned to him and asked a question I should have thought to ask before we'd left. "Where are we going?" I really hadn't cared before, but my curiosity was eating away at me.

"Ever been to Big Sur?"

"No, but I know where it is. It's like five hours away."

"More like six." He threw me a glance like he was expecting me to freak out. "I figured we'd stop and grab a motel along the way. There aren't any lights at night where we're going. We can set up camp tomorrow." He glanced at me again. "That okay with you?"

I nodded without giving him the satisfaction of meeting his gaze. I'd pulled off nonchalance well so far, so I couldn't give away just how nervous I'd become since suggesting—no, *begging*—to ride along with him.

We let the music fill the silence for the next half hour before I decided to speak again. I knew I was breaking our unspoken rule that we didn't have to talk.

Reaching forward, I turned the volume down to Nickelback's latest hit so Tobias could hear me. "Okay, I have to ask—and then I promise, no more talking unless you want to." I rushed to continue before I chickened out. "Since we're going to be together for an entire week, I need to know." *Shit. This could go badly.* "Is anything off limits?"

Confusion twisted his face before he spoke. "Um, I don't know. Are you planning on breaking the law? Is that the real reason you wanted to get out of town?"

I laughed, realizing how vague my question was. "God no. I meant are there any conversations that are off limits? Any *topics* I should be aware of? What about pet peeves?"

A smile tilted his mouth as he considered my words. "You mean like, should you avoid asking me why I dropped out of school? Or why my family is so fucked up?"

My heart drummed in my chest. That wasn't exactly how I'd seen our conversation going. "Um…" I frantically searched for the right words. But that was the problem—without knowing what had gone on with his family, I didn't know what to say. "That wasn't—"

He chuckled. "Relax. I don't have anything to hide."

I narrowed my eyes, ready to call his bluff. "You don't?"

He shrugged. "Nope." He met my eyes for a second before tightening his hands on the wheel and facing forward. "It's not me hiding stuff. It's my parents—and apparently Trin too. I didn't realize you were in the dark on this. I just assumed you knew."

Why is my heart beating so fast? "Assumed I knew what? What would they have to hide?"

I could feel the annoyance radiate from his body, and I could see that he was protecting them more than himself. But I didn't understand why.

"I'm adopted, Amelia."

My heart dropped to the floor of his truck. *What?*

"It's not a huge deal in the grand scheme of things, but my parents keeping it from me was pretty shitty."

"How did you find out? Did they tell you?"

He let out a laugh that was drowning in sarcasm. "I was looking into an international basketball tour and needed a passport. I was searching for my birth certificate in my dad's office, and that's when I found the adoption papers."

"Oh my God, Tobias. I had no idea."

He nodded. "When I confronted my parents, there was a big blowup. A lot of excuses, guilt trips, the works. Trinity had no clue what was going on at that point, but that's because I took off instead of dealing with it."

"You mean that's why you dropped out and no one knew where you'd gone?"

His jaw tensed as he gave a slight nod. "I was a bit of a wreck when I found out." His face reddened as if he were embarrassed to admit it. "I took off for months, missed the entire rest of the season and everything that came with in, including the recruiters who showed up just to see me. That was when the rumors started. Suddenly, I was the kid who had gotten into some trouble and took off to avoid the repercussions. To my parents, that story was way better than the real one, so they rolled with it."

My jaw dropped. "I remember that. Trinity was calling you every five seconds. I'd never seen her so worried. After you came back, she said you were in jail."

He scoffed as he shook his head. "Well, that was a lie."

I couldn't believe what I was hearing. "Then why didn't you say something? Everyone was talking about Malibu's golden boy going off the rails. Why would Trinity lie to me?"

"The last thing on my mind was correcting some stupid rumor floating around town. I don't even remember what I did during that week besides drive. But when I came home, my parents told Trinity what was really going on. They all decided that keeping up the family front was better than the truth."

"So they just let everyone think you committed some crime and landed in jail?"

"Yup. I couldn't say no. They offered me a deal I couldn't refuse."

"What was it?"

"If I kept quiet, they would tell me what they knew about my birth parents. I was eighteen, but I remember feeling so desperate to know who they were, why they'd given me up, that I accepted without looking for a better option. But the whole thing—it ate away at me."

"So you dropped out of school and gave up basketball?"

Tobias's jaw hardened, and his knuckles whitened with his grip. "I couldn't focus on anything. Finishing school became impossible. Basketball season was already over. The team hated me. My reputation was shot. I felt like I'd lost everything. Everything felt like a lie."

"I am so sorry. I feel awful for believing all the lies. I shouldn't have pried."

"You can ask me anything, Amelia." His eyes slipped to mine, but only for a second before returning to the long stretch of road before us. For the second time since I'd known him, I noticed his eye color—a smoky blue with a dark ring around the outer circle. I wished I could read the thoughts that lay beneath them. "Actually, it felt good to tell someone all that."

I swear the corner of his mouth lifted slightly, causing my heart to stutter. I couldn't remember the last time I'd seen Tobias James smile. Maybe when we were younger, when he'd just won a game of basketball, or when Trinity and I would get caught between the sprinklers late at night when we all should have been sleeping. But as he grew older, he'd become more guarded. His enjoyment had transitioned into competitiveness. And his playfulness had turned into expressions of confidence and intimidation.

"So," I started timidly, hoping to break the invisible barrier between us. "Does this mean we'll be talking more?"

He let out a breath of amusement. "I still like it quiet. I just want you to know it's not because I have anything to hide."

"Then why do you like the quiet?"

He shrugged. "I don't have that much to say anymore."

"Because you were lied to?"

"Because of what the lie did to me. Because of what I lost. I used to have things to talk about. I was driven and passionate about basketball and school. I didn't even see it all slipping away from me until it was gone. And now"—he shrugged—"nothing feels like it was ever really mine, not even basketball."

My breath caught in my throat as an ache sliced through my chest. As much as I wanted to, I couldn't tell him that wasn't true. It wasn't my place.

"Anyway," Tobias said, cutting into my thoughts and tightening his grip on the wheel. "I don't mean to bore you. But I figured we'd get that out of the way."

I couldn't even begin to imagine how I would cope with finding out I was adopted. To find out I'd been given up, and then lied to by my adopted parents my whole life. It would probably change me too.

My thoughts wandered through the new silence, this one heavier, but not from discomfort. I knew I had the freedom to ask everything I'd been curious about over the months, but I was afraid to know all the answers.

For the next three hours, I chose to stay in that silence, where it was safer.

"I wanted to enter the draft after one year of college," he said like he'd been thinking about it for a long time.

My head snapped so hard in his direction, I could feel the tailwind of the breeze I'd created. "Don't you have to finish college to enter the draft?"

"Not always. They have development leagues in the NBA. It's still pro ball, just on a smaller scale. I could train there then eventually trade up." He cocked an eyebrow like he knew he was speaking a different language to me. "Trading up is like transitioning from minor leagues to major leagues."

"Oh." I relaxed my shoulders against the seat, my breath leaving me in a long, steady stream. "I'm sure it's not too late."

"Even if it's not, I'm a little rusty."

"You haven't played at all?"

He shook his head. "I haven't even touched a ball."

I tried to compare his love for basketball to my dancing. I couldn't imagine going a single day without moving to some type of rhythm, even if it was just the sound of rain tapping against my bedroom window. To give that up the way he'd given up basketball was the stuff of tragedies.

When I looked at him again, I felt a deep tug in my gut and a warmth spreading outward as I realized that the boy I was suddenly crushing on had always been there. I had just never seen him, not *really*.

"It's funny," I said with a laugh. "Remember when Trin and I used to make up those stupid dances while you and your buddies played ball at the community court?"

He chuckled. "How could I forget? While the guys were distracted by your miniskirts, I'd steal the ball and dunk the shit out of it. Those *stupid* dances won me a lot of games."

"Ha. Yeah, well, I still dream of being an NBA dancer thanks to those times."

"Then I'm sure your dreams will come true."

I frowned before shaking my head. "I don't know. It's not like basketball. I'd have to try out for every team I'm interested in, and since auditions are usually around the same time each summer, I'll have to choose a select few. But I've always dreamed of dancing for the LA Lions." I felt my cheeks heat, but I didn't understand why. I'd never been embarrassed of my big dreams. Except this time, I'd already been turned down by them once because of my age. "And the Lions will only have a few spots available when it comes time to audition."

Tobias wrinkled his face in confusion. "There are thirty-something dancers on a squad."

Of course he would know how many girls were on the Lions dance team. "Yeah, but most of the girls will be returning from last season."

"Ah, I see."

"But it doesn't matter if I get picked. Dancing at Gravity opens so many doors in the industry. I'm just waiting until I graduate to begin the audition process."

The silence that followed made me focus on the darkness that had fallen over us since the start of our trip. It was dark when we pulled into a motel parking lot just outside of Monterey County.

Tobias pulled his keys out of the ignition. "Another hour to go in the morning."

There was really nothing to the place. It had a flickering neon

Vacancy sign out front, and wrought iron rimmed the pool that sat off to one side. It was dingy but fine for a short night's sleep. I wasn't anxious to be anywhere anytime soon.

"Oh. Here." I reached into my purse to give him my credit card, but he stopped my hand before I could pull it out of my bag.

"This is on me."

I wasn't sure how I felt about him paying for our room, but I knew better than to argue. There were other ways I could contribute to our trip, I would just have to figure out what they were.

Our room looked no better than the exterior. The floral comforter appeared ancient in style, and the vertical blinds added to the ambience as they flapped from the breeze of the AC unit tapered against the wall.

"Have you stayed here before?"

He was setting down my bags on the bed when I asked.

"The front desk lady called you Tobias when you walked up."

He shrugged. "This is my usual stop on my way to where we're going."

"To the campground?"

He shrugged, almost shyly. "Something like that." He took a step back toward the door. "I'm going to grab the rest of the stuff from the truck. We don't need it tonight, but I don't exactly trust the people wandering around here, hence the one room instead of two." He gestured to the bed. "I'd sleep in my truck, but—"

"Don't be ridiculous." I squinted, hoping I wasn't making the situation any more awkward than it had started out. "I'm fine with sharing. As long as you're okay with naked spooning. It's the only way I'll sleep."

The glare he shot me next split my smile into a full-blown grin.

"You know," he started. "I wouldn't be surprised if you were telling the truth right now. You're a bold one, Amelia Clark. And persistent. I should worry that you do this with everyone—taking off on week-long road trips, offering to share dirty motel beds... while spooning naked, no less."

I threw my head back and laughed. It wasn't until I met his eyes again that my amusement settled. "I promise you're the only one, Tobias James."

The half smile that lit his face next shouldn't have made my insides dance and my neck feel hot. It should have made me realize what was happening right then and there. Tobias and I were just at the start of our trip together, and we were already flirting. Worst of all, I didn't want it to stop.

Chapter 6

TOBIAS

I should have known where things were headed between us on that very first night when I brought the rest of our things into the motel and Amelia was in the shower. It was as if I'd been possessed earlier in the day when I'd run to the grocery store before picking Amelia up for our trip. At the store, my first stop had been the bakery section. I'd picked out a fancy cupcake to give to Amelia for her birthday.

She was wrapped in a towel when I presented it to her. The flame of the single candle flickered against the dimness of the room. Her jaw dropped, and her hand loosened from the towel. She must not have had time to completely knot it, because it unraveled almost instantly.

"Shit," she squealed as one hand flew to cover the section between her thighs.

I was unashamed by my admiration and enamored by her shape— her golden skin, the way her thick hips curved deep into her waist, and her abs that tightened and released in quick time as my eyes slid like water droplets over every inch.

Fuck me. Up until that point, I could have vividly remembered the last time I'd seen a woman naked. But after seeing Amelia standing there, shower sweat glistening on her skin, I knew beyond a shadow of a doubt she was the most beautiful woman in existence.

My gaze traced her lean, athletic build, admiring her tiny waist, thick hips, and natural breasts. Her breasts weren't large by any means, but I knew they could easily fill my palms. I wondered how sensitive those light-brown nipples would be if I plucked them with my teeth.

For a brief, perverted second, I imagined the slip of the towel hadn't been an accident. I imagined dropping to my knees and inhaling her like she was fine wine.

"Take the damn cupcake," she squealed, snapping me from my daydream.

If I hadn't been eating her out in my mind, I would have realized why she wasn't covering herself up completely. "Oh shit." I jumped forward and snatched the cupcake away, freeing her hands to swoop down and rewrap her towel, securing it tightly over her heaving chest.

"Oh my God," she said while opening her eyes wide at me. "You just saw me naked."

"I did," I confirmed with a slow nod. "Sorry I didn't react faster, but I—"

She growled, cutting me off and pushing past me to get to her bags. "Don't even try. There's no erasing that from your memory, I'm sure."

"Definitely not." When I chuckled, guilt settled in. "For what it's worth, you have nothing to be embarrassed about."

"I'm not embarrassed about my body. I don't usually give free shows away. Something like that needs to be earned, ya know?"

I bit my lip, hesitating before blurting out the first thing that came to mind. "C'mon, Amelia. It's not like you did it on purpose."

"But you *looked* on purpose."

I laughed. "Well, yeah, maybe so. But in all fairness, I was caught off guard. Next time, I'll look away faster."

Her expression revealed absolute horror. "Next time? No, Tobias. The next man who gets to see me naked will put in the work first."

"Well, maybe you can wish for just that."

Her face twisted in confusion. "Huh?"

I held up the cupcake again while pulling the lighter from my back pocket. After relighting the candle, I smiled at her through the flame. "It's time to make a wish, Birthday Girl."

Chapter 7

AMELIA

Tobias let me sleep past the alarm he'd set for us. I didn't know why, but my exhausted body thanked him for it. I'd had too much on my mind lately, graduation being the tip of the iceberg, but last night, the man sleeping beside me weighed on my thoughts too.

The way he'd looked at me after my towel slipped, like he could have taken me right there, scared me as much as it thrilled me. But more than anything, it was the gesture with the birthday cupcake that had thrown me. I would have never pegged him as the sweet-and-thoughtful type.

It turned out there were more dimensions to Tobias James than I'd ever dared to think about.

"Ready to hit the road, Birthday Girl?"

I tied my sneaker laces and stood up with a slap of my thighs. "Yup. You're going to keep calling me that, aren't you?"

"Yup."

I rolled my eyes. At least he'd stopped calling me Kid. "Should we stop for food?"

He opened the hotel door to let me walk through first. "I went shopping before we left. I think I grabbed all your favorite things."

I slowed in my tracks as I glanced at him over my shoulder, amused. "And how would you know what my favorite things are?"

He shrugged. "You've been rummaging around my kitchen for years. And I'm a dude. I notice when food goes missing. Extra-toasted Cheez-Its, beef jerky, mixed nuts, avocados, Fuji apples, and grapefruit Perrier. That about sum it up?"

My cheeks felt hot from surprise. "Sure, those are some of my favorite snacks. But none of that is breakfast. I need a real meal."

"Cinnamon Toast Crunch?" he asked. "I bought that too."

My mouth fell open. "You did?"

He nodded. "And that Lactaid milk you love."

"It's so good. And lactose free."

His lip pulled up at the corner. "You're so weird."

45

"And what do *you* eat for breakfast, Mr. Judgy?"

"I'll give you one guess." He lifted a Styrofoam cup to his lips and sipped slowly.

I wrinkled my nose. "That's it? Just coffee? How does that fill you up?"

"I add butter."

"And I'm the weird one?"

He chuckled. "Don't knock it until you've tried it."

"I think I'll take my chances." I flipped my head around to focus on walking through the parking lot. "Cereal it is. I'll even do your truck this one solid and leave it dry."

We arrived at the truck just then, and he reached around me to open the door. When he leaned in to whisper in my ear from behind, my entire body felt as if he'd just lit it on fire. "Thanks, smart-ass."

I managed to avoid his eyes for the next hour as we wound our way through mountainous terrain, and I felt surprisingly calm. I hadn't thought much about what to expect this coming week, figuring anything different from the mundane would be exactly what my soul was craving. There was so much more to see beyond the mirrored walls of the dance studio and the bluish-green waves that washed onto the Malibu beach. I'd never considered that anything was lacking from my life until my options became so limited I couldn't even see past them.

Tobias and I continued to climb the deserted road until nothing was left around us. The clearing was wide, overlooking a rugged and mountainous section where the Santa Lucia Mountains rose abruptly from the Pacific Ocean.

"Where are we?" I felt his amused eyes on me at my question. I shook my head and tried again. "I mean, I know *where* we are. But what is this place?"

"It's exactly what you see. An empty lot. That's pretty much it."

"And this is where you spend your time when you leave Malibu?"

He shrugged. "Mostly, yeah. I love it up here." He nodded toward the edge of the cliff. "It's peaceful, private, filled with endless possibilities, you know?"

"Like a blank canvas. Or should I say an empty court?"

He frowned as if he found my pun annoying. "Something like that." He turned to look at me. "What would you do with this space if it were yours?"

My hesitation didn't come from a lack of ideas. I had so many, I couldn't sort through them fast enough. "Build on it, I suppose."

"Really?" His curiosity was filled with passion. "What would you build?"

My heart thumped a little bit harder. "Is this a trick question?"

He chuckled. "No, not at all. I've been asking myself the same thing since this place became mine. It would be nice to get a different take on it."

I swallowed before sneaking a glance at Tobias. "Since it became yours?" I looked back out at the sight before me, more stunned than before. "How?"

"I purchased it after the whole adoption thing came to light. Used my entire trust fund. Every time I come here, I brainstorm what I could do with it."

My chest grew heavy with his confession. "You still haven't decided?"

He shook his head, his jaw firm. "Maybe nothing. Sometimes I wonder if changing it will destroy its beauty. There's nothing wrong with it as is."

Something about his words made me wonder if he compared the land to his own situation. Did he wish he'd never found out about the adoption? Did he wish he'd never *been* adopted? I didn't dare ask those questions.

"I see your dilemma," I finally said.

"Do you?"

Our eyes met, clicking together like they'd always belonged that way. "I do. There's no reason to rush a decision like that. It seems you appreciate it all the same."

His eyes softened, crinkling slightly at the corners. "Want the tour?"

♥

The "tour" consisted of a walk around the perimeter of the property— well, as much property as we could walk on without falling off the cliff— and then setting up a large tent in which Tobias placed a folding table, some chairs, the two coolers he'd brought, and our bags.

By the time we were all set up, my stomach was growling from a missed meal. It was well past lunchtime but not quite time for dinner.

"I don't think the snacks you brought will hold me over. I need some real sustenance."

Tobias checked the time on his phone. "Let's head into town. We can grab an early dinner, and if you want to grab more things at the store, we can stop there too."

"Deal."

The ride into town was only fifteen minutes from where we'd set up camp, and we wasted no time finding the restaurant he had described. It was a small establishment on the corner of a row of aged brick buildings, dimly lit inside by large, glass-encased candlesticks. Jazz music streamed through the small black speakers secured to the corners of the room. It seemed like a place where couples would spend first dates and anniversaries, not a quick meal between two people who had barely ever spoken.

I tilted my head and stared at him a little funny, and he returned it with an amused smile.

"What are you looking at me like that for?" he asked.

I shrugged and took a sip of my water. "Nothing." I dared another glance at him as the liquid slid down my throat. I could feel its crisp bite as it grazed its way into my chest as it hit me for the millionth time that day just how annoyingly attractive Tobias was.

"C'mon, Amelia. You can't hold back if we're going to be together for an entire week. No secrets."

If I'd known our trip would consist of me learning just how deep one's blush could get, I probably would have stayed home and moped with pleasure all week long. How was it that in the years I'd known Tobias James, I'd never once looked at him this way?

"Okay, fine." I sighed. "This place—I would have never pictured you here. I mean, there's nothing wrong with it. I guess I'm used to seeing you all greased up from head to toe from working on your truck."

His eyes lit with his laugh. "In my defense, the grease doesn't cover *all* of my body. Just the exposed parts."

That joke deserved the hard eye roll it received. "Thank you for that mental picture."

"What are you picturing exactly?"

In seconds, I'd balled the cloth napkin into my palm and chucked it across the table, unable to contain my laughter. "Enough. That's like, the third crude joke you've made this trip, and it's barely been twenty-four hours."

His head tilted. "Three? You sure? I can only recall two."

I sighed dramatically and averted my eyes. "And yesterday when you saw me..." I cleared my throat to mask my nonresponse.

His eyes narrowed. "Oh no, I didn't make any jokes last night. I was a complete gentleman. I even bought you a cupcake."

I opened then closed my mouth, realizing I had no argument. Flustered, I accepted my napkin, which he held toward me, then slammed it in my lap. "See? That right there is a perfect example of what I'm talking about. Since when did you become the thoughtful one around here? Helping me with my tire. Driving me to LA just so I could make it to an audition. Letting me come with you to your secret hideaway. Taking me to a nice dinner at a fancy restaurant."

He leaned in when I was done. The table between us was so small, his face landed mere inches from mine. "And you thought I was, what? An asshole grease monkey with awful taste in food?"

My cheeks burned. That wasn't what I'd thought at all—I don't think—but when I opened my mouth to speak, I couldn't seem to form the right words.

The corner of his mouth ticked up so quick I almost missed it. "Be careful, Birthday Girl. I might just continue to surprise you." He winked, causing the heat low in my belly to spread.

He blinked nice and slow, the gravelly tone of his voice leaving a lingering impression in my chest. I'd have to work on tuning him out, visually and audibly.

"It's not my birthday anymore." My smug reminder only made me feel good for a second.

He shrugged, unfazed. "Maybe not, but that doesn't mean we can't celebrate all week long."

A laugh burst from my throat. "Don't be ridiculous. You can't keep this chivalry up for a full week."

His eyes darkened. "I can't?"

My throat went dry just as his gaze slipped down from my face. It was only for a moment, but I could feel his stare like a burning torch against my skin. *I'm imagining it.* Clearly, my crush on my best friend's brother had fried my brain to the point of imagining he actually wanted me. It was ridiculous to even entertain the idea. Tobias was unquestionably hot, but I wasn't on this trip to fall in love with my best friend's brother. And I knew better than to think he wanted anything from me.

I leaned back, distancing myself from the mirage in front of me. "Okay. Keep up the chivalry if you want to. Maybe I'll survive this week after all."

A dimple indented his left cheek. "I wouldn't get your hopes up."

"Ugh," I groaned. "How about you humor me, at least until dessert?"

His eyes widened as I registered how well I'd just set him up for another joke. I held up a hand and bowed my head to hide my blush. "Forget I said that, please." I pulled the menu from the table and opened it. "How about you tell me what you recommend?"

His lips twitched into a half smile. "Everything. What are you in the mood for? Besides dessert?"

My lips pinched together as I suppressed an eyeroll. "Steak."

"Then get the ribeye. Medium. With the garlic mash on the side. It's incredible."

I decided against the garlic mashed potatoes. The last thing I wanted was for Tobias to get a whiff of my herb-infested breath while we were smashed against each other in the back of his truck. Not that I cared if the stench of my breath annoyed him. It was more of a courtesy thing. He'd let me come along. I at least owed him good breath. I ordered the feta Brussels sprouts instead.

Once the waitress took our order, our conversation moved into safer territory. He asked me about dance, and I asked him about working at the garage. Innocent, friendly banter. If only we could keep it there.

"So," I said once our food was sitting in front of us. "You mentioned not knowing what to do with the land. What have you considered?" As I stabbed another piece of ribeye and brought it to my mouth, I tried my best to act nonchalant. I didn't want to make him feel like this was an interrogation, but my curiosity wouldn't let up. Clearly, Tobias kept to himself for a reason. Knowing what I knew now, I feared that reason was trust. And for some strange reason, I wanted him to trust me.

He reached for his water then eased it to his mouth. In a single slow blink, his eyes locked on mine like he was assessing me. For all I knew, he was debating whether he should trust me. Why did that terrify me?

"Honestly, I can only think of what I *don't* want to do to that space."

"What's that?"

The teasing smile that spread across his mouth next was so shocking,

I almost missed his words. "Build on it."

It took a few seconds for my memory to catch up with his words. His bluish-gray eyes sparkled as his smile deepened knowingly since that was exactly what I'd suggested hours ago. My heart sped at the beauty of it all. I couldn't remember the last time I'd seen him smile, but I knew I liked it.

"Whatever I do, I want to keep it open, minimal. Don't get me wrong, I'm not against a busy lifestyle, but when I come here, it's to get away from the hustle and bustle. Do you ever want to get away?" He stared imploringly into my eyes. "From expectations, distractions, and obligations. Don't you ever just want to turn it off?"

"Yes." The answer came quickly and left me almost breathless, catching me off guard. I'd always been a happy person, the life of the party, easy to get along with. My life was stress free for the most part. But the full day I'd spent with Tobias James had made me realize how much I'd misidentified the perspective I had on my life.

Life was full of expectations.

Of greed.

Of power.

Nothing was possible without money.

And if one didn't have money, power, and things, she was criticized for it. At least that was what I'd experienced in my eighteen years of living. I'd grown accustomed to all sorts of things that didn't make me feel safe inside. That had thrown me off balance. It was one of the main reasons I drove over two hours a day, five days a week, to take dance classes in LA. It was there I found all the things I'd been lacking at home. At Gravity, I felt free of all the bullshit I'd been taught over the years. I'd begun to gain a new perspective, one I craved more and more.

I'd been lost in my own thoughts so deeply, it took a second to register the new expression on Tobias's face. His curiosity shone brightly beneath the large flickering candle that hung above our heads, and his long, dark hair gleamed in the light. I didn't care that it looked wild and tangled from the mountain winds, that his full lips looked plump and chapped from the sun, or that his smile was a little crooked when he braved one.

Just sharing a small space with Tobias James showed me a new perspective to life, one that didn't add up to most people, especially to people like my parents. Tobias had the opportunity to be whatever— *who*ever—he wanted to be. But that wasn't what he'd chosen. Instead, he'd chosen adventure. And in that moment, I kind of fell in love with him for it.

Okay, so *love* was kind of a strong word for how I felt. Our connection was clearly strong and our attraction inevitable. But love? I still barely knew the guy except for the vibes he put off and what he'd already told me about himself. He was a big ball of mystery, although I wouldn't call him complicated, just… lost.

And Trinity would kill me for being interested in him. *Why do I keep forgetting?*

"Ready to head back?" he asked.

I'd finished my steak and had just been guzzling water while staring curiously into his eyes. "Ready if you are."

He tossed his napkin onto the table and stood, holding out his hand to me when he did. "I have a tab here."

I looked at his hand. It was large and calloused. There was nothing pretty about it. But for some reason, I was eager to feel it wrapped around mine. I placed my hand in his, shivering slightly at the touch and letting him pull me to my feet, all the while knowing I was being ridiculous—I couldn't let my attraction move past where it had already gone. But the more I seemed to think about not having Tobias James, the more I wanted him, the more I craved him, and the more I couldn't let go of my curiosity.

I walked alongside him, feeling as good as I had that one time I'd sneaked a few sips of my mom's champagne. I was drunk off Tobias's proximity, and I never wanted the feeling to end.

As he opened the passenger door of his truck to let me in, I turned around and tilted my chin up to look him directly in the eyes and said exactly what I was thinking in that moment.

"Maybe this was a bad idea."

He nodded, his eyes smoldering like they were burning their way right through me. "I tried to warn you, Birthday Girl. No turning back now."

Chapter 8

TOBIAS

She's my little sister's best friend. That mental reminder should have stopped my raging hard-on in its tracks by the time we arrived back on the lot. But knowing how wrong my feelings were only made me want her more.

The resistance I'd felt when she had first asked to come on the trip hit me hard when I started setting up the bed of my pickup for us to sleep. Sure, we'd managed to spend an entire night together in a hotel room without anything happening, but that didn't mean I didn't *want* anything to happen.

The gray and red tent was almost as tall as me and customized to fit the back of my truck. The mattress was firm, fitting snugly against the walls around us. Between all the blankets Amelia had brought and all the pillows I had brought, our sleeping area looked like a legit porno shoot.

On second thought, my mind had possibly gone to "porno shoot" after seeing Amelia's sleeping attire.

She walked out of the big tent wearing shorts and a tank top. The outfit was hardly porno material, but when she crawled onto the bed of my truck, I may have had a dirty thought or twenty.

She wasn't wearing a bra, not that I was trying to notice. I wasn't. But it was a little difficult not to when she walked into our sleep space with the heat lamp directly over her tight white tank, calling attention to her tits like a fucking lighthouse.

I need to get my head out of the gutter.

"I need to buy a sweater tomorrow," she said. "I didn't realize how cold it would get up here."

Don't look. Don't look.

"We can go first thing."

"Thanks," she said with a sigh. Then she pointed to the bed. "Which side is yours?"

I bit the inside of my lip to keep from smiling. "I sleep in the middle, usually, so either side is fine."

She quirked a brow, and I already knew where the conversation was headed. "Really, so you've never brought a girl out here?"

I ground my teeth at the reminder. "Nah. You're the first stubborn one who wouldn't take no for an answer."

She returned my asshole comment with a glare. "Too bad." She nodded toward the bed. "This is, like, the optimal sex pad."

Something about how nonchalantly she said "sex pad" tensed my shoulders. "I didn't realize you were so experienced."

Her blush deepened. "I'm not. But a guy like you—"

I put my palm in the air, facing her. "I'm going to stop you there before that mouth of yours says something you'll regret. You did a stellar job of not pissing me off today, and I might actually enjoy having you around. So can you get into this bed and shut the hell up?"

She let out a small breath before narrowing her eyes. "What makes you think I'd respond to that kind of request?"

I batted my eyes at her. My chest was on the verge of exploding from the pressure. "Please."

A half growl, half scream slipped past her lips before she pushed past me toward the bed.

I followed her lead, crawling under the beige comforter and turning to the opposite side so our asses were facing each other. I couldn't risk accidently rubbing against her when just her presence made me spring to life like a prepubescent boy.

"I wasn't going to say anything bad."

"Huh?" I grumbled, confused by what she was talking about.

"When I said 'a guy like you,' I didn't mean it in a bad way."

"Then how did you mean it?"

"It's just… I remember how popular you were in high school. It's not like you had trouble with the ladies. I mean, I wouldn't have called you a player or anyth—"

"I'm not a player. Never was."

Her head snapped to find my eyes over her shoulder. "Th-that's what I said."

She was right, but something about her words—just the fact that she'd thought about me being a player or not—pissed me the hell off.

If I'm angry, then why am I sporting a boner the size of Texas?

Amelia was nothing like anyone I'd ever dated before. She was young. She was good. And I wasn't the kind of guy who did "good" well.

"You should probably stop talking before that mouth of yours gets you in trouble."

She laughed softly. "Damn, okay, but only after you tell me why you haven't brought anyone else here."

I wasn't about to let her be the only one to ask questions.

"Sure," I finally said. "But then you have to answer a question for me."

"Deal."

I smiled at the ease with which she agreed, and a sick part of me wanted to see how far I could push it. I wouldn't, though. I stood by what I'd told her. Just because I'd been a bit of a flirt in high school didn't mean I had dated every chick who'd walked by me. A few girls stuck out in my mind, but none of them had ever lasted more than a few months. And that wasn't because I'd gotten bored and tossed them, or cheated, or done any of that shit. It was because basketball had always come first, and no one had understood that except me.

"Contrary to what most people believe, I didn't date much in high school or even college. I was focused on basketball, and that didn't leave much time for girls. And this past year has been about other things. No chicks allowed."

"I'm a chick."

I bit my lip to keep from laughing. I didn't want Amelia to know just how much I was enjoying her company. "Yeah, well. You don't count. You're safe."

The silence that came next felt far too heavy. Maybe I should have quit while I was ahead.

"Good to know." She flipped her body so her back was facing me. "Well, thank you for letting me crash your trip." Her tone was quieter, almost apologetic.

I frowned. "Hey." There was a tightening in my chest. I should have never told her she didn't count or that she was safe, because neither of those things was true.

When she didn't turn back around or speak, I slid closer, until my lips could reach her ear. I felt her entire body tense beside mine. "For what it's worth, I'm glad you were my first."

Light laughter floated from Amelia's throat. Her body shook slightly, and my mouth pulled into a slow smile. I could get used to that sound, to the way her body moved, to her warmth, to this feeling.

I felt myself start to doze off when the sleep-filled rasp of her voice shocked me completely still.

"You say that like maybe I'm not so safe after all."

If I hadn't considered Amelia dangerous before, I certainly did then. She wasn't anything like I'd expected. Even after all these years—of living so close to her, of hearing her giggle with my sister in the bedroom next to mine, of ignoring her as she chased my sister around the pool in her tiny red bikini—I hadn't given much thought to my sister's best friend. But in the span of one week, everything had changed.

Everything.

Chapter 9

AMELIA

"Do you see yourself playing basketball again?"

We were sitting on a set of chairs near the edge of the bluff while eating our breakfast when I decided to ask the question I'd feared asking yesterday. If there was one thing I understood about Tobias, it was the level of commitment he had for basketball. But more than that, I understood his passion. He carried a basketball the way I executed a jazz walk, with enough confidence to intimidate most.

"Didn't we talk about this yesterday? I messed up, remember?"

"Jeez, Tobias. You took a year off. You're only nineteen. It's not like you're forty."

"You don't get it. Abandoning my team doesn't exactly help my chances. I didn't even defer school or anything. I just quit."

He'd given up before he'd even really tried.

"So that's it? No more basketball? Ever?" I didn't care how incredulous my tone sounded. He should know how ridiculous he was being. "You don't just give up on your dreams, Tobias. Not when you've worked your entire life. And not when you're as talented as you are. You have a gift most wish they had even a smidge of. Don't waste it."

"Well, thanks, but it's not that simple. I don't even remember what it's like to hold a ball."

"I don't believe that."

"It doesn't matter, Amelia. I'd be rusty as hell and in need of some serious training before even considering it."

"Then pick up a damn ball."

He chuckled in a way that weighed heavily in my chest. I wouldn't let him give up on himself. I couldn't. But I didn't understand why Tobias had to be so stubborn. What would it take for him to remember what it felt like to fly down that court and take that buzzer shot from the fifty just in time to break the tie and win the game?

Maybe this was my purpose in Tobias's life—and my reason for going on this trip—to help him rekindle his love for the game and to somehow get him to hold a ball in his hands again.

"You're cute when you're angry. You know that?"

My entire body heated at his words, and I just knew my face had turned red. "Don't change the subject. You don't get to avoid this." My eyes caught on his truck, and an idea sparked. "Tell me you have a ball with you."

He hesitated, and I knew the answer before he even responded.

I smiled, my lips spreading wide. "Let's go to a court today. I'm sure there's one nearby."

"You're serious?"

"Dead serious."

He sighed, and his head lolled behind him before straightening again. "All right, Birthday Girl. Your wish is my command. But you'll need to do something for me in return."

I squealed and jumped in my chair, feeling the cold splash of milk and cereal hit my chest and drip between my breasts. "Shit." I reached for a napkin just as Tobias handed one to me.

His eyes connected with mine. "You need to dance for me."

"What?"

He laughed and shrugged. "If I'm going to play ball, then you're going to dance."

♥

As we drove off in the truck to find a basketball court, I had to fight hard with myself to ignore how tired and achy I was from a restless sleep. But by the sound of Tobias's breathing during the night, I was certain he'd had just as much trouble as me.

We passed through the ranger station, and he paid them at the entrance, then we drove in about a mile until we reached a sandy clearing that overlooked the ocean.

"Here it is. And we can shower when we're done." He pulled on his door handle to get out of the truck. "Don't worry. There's hot water."

That's a relief.

He pointed to a small fenced-in area with a showerhead looming over the top of it, but I only glanced at it before my eye caught on Tobias spinning the basketball on his middle finger. He was standing just outside the driver's side, and his eyes were directly on me, brows perked. "You ready?"

I turned toward my door before he could see my smile. "As I'll ever be."

Tobias led the way, and I couldn't help but run my eyes down his frame. He was so tall and defined. The year off hadn't hurt him in that department. And I doubted it had hurt him in any other department either. It would just take getting him on the court to show him. Because if he were anything like me, the moment he got a taste of what he'd been missing, he would want more of it.

There was a fine line between passion and obsession. Tobias and I—we had both.

"So, what are we doing, Birthday Girl? A game of Horse? Pig? Around the World? You name it."

I wrinkled my nose and shook my head. "None of the above. We're playing a real game. Half court. You said you were rusty, which means I have a chance."

He laughed a boisterous laugh, one that reached my insides, slid down my core, and curled my toes. It had been a long time since I'd heard that laugh. I didn't know it was possible to miss something I'd never even realized existed before.

"All right." He started a slow dribble, circling me as he did, watching me curiously. "We'll play to twenty. And when it's over, I want to see you dance. Full out. I'll pick the song."

I rolled my eyes but shrugged, giving in to his demands. That was a challenge I had no problem accepting. "Let's see your moves, hot shot."

He grinned so wide, I could see a sliver of gums around the bright white of his teeth. "You realize the guys I used to play with were over a foot taller than you, right? Your challenge is cute and all, but are you sure you want to do this?"

His teasing lit a fire in me, one that made me smile back just as hard. "Maybe I should level the playing field." My arms crossed at the hem of my tank top and grabbed the material at the bottom. With one pull, I whipped my shirt off and tossed it toward the sidelines, revealing my black sports bra. I brought my fists to my hips before glancing back at Tobias.

His eyes were narrowed on mine. "Really?"

My smile turned smug. "Yup." I reached toward him, swiped the ball from his hold, and dribbled my way toward half court.

He didn't go easy on me, staying on my ass as I tried to take the ball toward the basket, stealing the ball at every opportunity, towering over me, and making it impossible for me to make a shot. But he didn't play his hardest either. His three-pointers were effortless, barely ever touching the rim as they went down. He even gave me a good show by throwing in a few layups and dunks.

Unfortunately, I was too impressed to be annoyed by his exhibition.

"Twenty to zero. Time for that dance." He held the ball in the air and sauntered to his truck.

"You're ten times my size, and you couldn't even let me have one?" I'd known I wasn't going to win, but the jerk hadn't even taken pity on me. "That's what some would call a bully." I folded my arms across my chest and glared at him.

He chuckled and stared at his phone as he scrolled through it. I didn't know what he was doing until a song started streaming through his truck speakers. I was already covered in sweat. While he'd walked the entire game, I'd been running my ass off.

"No whining, Birthday Girl. Besides, you still owe me an I-O-U."

I laughed. "I forgot about that."

When I recognized the song "Swish Swish" by Katy Perry, I folded my arms across my chest and glared. "Clever."

"No more sass from you," he said with a snap of his fingers. "Dance, monkey."

I did my best to ignore his cocky grin and his bright grayish-blues that were locked on me as I transitioned my focus to the music. By the end of the second eight-count, I was completely in the zone.

The tone of my every movement was filled with all the sass I felt inside me—some flowy steps followed by clean pops and quick footwork—all perfectly following the lyrics. The song was flirty, fun, and I was able to recover from my disastrous performance playing basketball. And Tobias wasn't taking his eyes off me.

WATCH: SWISH SWISH
smarturl.it/Defying_SwishSwish

I broke out of character about halfway through the song and jogged over to Tobias. Grabbing his hands, I tried to pull him to his feet, but he fought back, laughing. "What are you doing?"

"I played ball with you, now you have to dance with me."

"Not even if hell freezes over. I don't dance, Birthday Girl."

"C'mon. It's just us out here. You owe me."

He shook his head and held his hands in the air. "I don't owe you a thing. We made a deal, and we both honored that deal. I'm not dancing with you."

I pouted, but not even that could convince him. Instead, he hopped off the truck and handed me my small bag I'd brought for the shower. "Time to wash up. We'll head back up for lunch. Maybe I'll show you how to play cards next."

He was several strides ahead of me by the time I started moving. "How do you always do that?" I asked when I caught up to him.

"Do what?"

"Find a way to change the subject entirely. Coming here was about you remembering why you loved basketball."

He glanced at me, his brows pulled together. "I already remember why I loved shooting hoops. And I have to admit"—he tossed the ball from one hand to the other—"I miss holding the ball. I miss the rush of the game, the pandemonium in the crowds, and hearing my name being chanted by hundreds of fans. I miss winning. Hell, I even miss losing."

Something quickened in my chest when I thought that was all he was going to give me. "So then what's the problem? Why not go for it again?"

He sighed and dropped his head back. "A year in this game is a long time to be away from it."

"You've already given me that excuse," I challenged.

"I can't just jump in like I never left."

My eyes narrowed. "Not good enough."

His expression softened. "I didn't lose sight of my dreams, Amelia. Life got hard, and I quit. No one respects a quitter."

"See, that's where you and I will continue to disagree. You didn't quit, Tobias. Your focus was on basketball your entire life. Learning what you did…" I paused, afraid to continue and word things the wrong way. "I can't imagine what you went through learning about your family like that. You did what you did for yourself because it was what you needed at the time. You took a break. There's nothing wrong with taking a time out. Even the best players get benched. It doesn't mean you give up. It means you go back out there and try harder."

Tobias stopped in his tracks, and his face twisted into something resembling a smile and confusion. "Did you just pep talk me?"

I laughed, happy he'd taken my verbal scolding well. "I guess I did."

"Well then, coach, it's time to hit the showers." He pointed at the fenced-in faucet. "Who goes first? Or should we do this together?" His smile tipped into a grin. "You know, as a team?"

"Nice try, hot shot." I stepped around him, peeked over my shoulder, and smiled. *Two can play this game.* "I'll go first just in case there's only enough hot water for one. Something tells me you won't mind taking a cold one."

Chapter 10

TOBIAS

ucking showers. I never thought I would hate them as much as I did that week. Amelia and I had a routine. We would eat breakfast, play ball, I would watch her dance, then we would shower before heading back to camp. The rest of the day wasn't as scheduled. We rotated between hiking, playing cards, and driving into town for a change of scenery.

Our time together was surprisingly effortless. She made me laugh, something I couldn't remember doing in a long-ass time. And after the first night, I'd started to sleep well beside her—not without a raging hard-on, but hey, I was proud I'd been able to keep it to myself.

But those fucking showers. They killed me in the worst way, giving me just a glimpse of Amelia's perfect bronze skin from her shoulders up, and each day only worsened my suffering. She was becoming harder to resist, to the point I'd forgotten why I was resisting.

She's your sister's best friend.

She's still in high school.

You're no good for her.

Three loud thoughts always came through, reminding me why I needed to keep my dick in my pants and my mouth away from all the places it wanted to kiss. And those thoughts were cycling through my mind that night as we lay on our backs, staring up at the roof of the tent.

"Two days left," she said quietly, breaking through our heavy silence.

I turned my head to face her, loving the way the moonlight spotlighted her profile. "Are you ready to go back?"

Our eyes locked as she shook her head. "No."

I couldn't hold back, not when just the shift of her body scented the air with her green-apple after-shower spray. It was a fragrance I knew would never leave me along with so many other memories of Amelia I'd accumulated over our week together. The log in my head was long, the capacity endless.

I took her hand in mine, weaving my fingers between hers. The move was innocent enough, but we both knew it was anything but. It was her move now. She could pull away at any moment. That would be enough to tell me "no."

When I felt the squeeze of her small fingers around mine, I sucked in a breath I hadn't meant for her to hear. *Shit.*

"You okay?" Her voice was soft and filled with an ache I wanted to mend.

I definitely wasn't okay. How the hell was it that I'd completely forgotten how to flirt with a girl? It had come so easily to me before.

There's been no one like Amelia Clark, you jackass.

I turned my body to face her, somewhat awkwardly as I got tangled up in the sheets and comforter. Once I finally escaped the mess, I peered back into her watchful eyes. "Do you, um, need another pillow?"

Before she could respond, I reached for the one between us and slid it around her waist. "Here." Her body was firm but curvy enough to give my eyes nice terrain to wander across when she was in those little dance outfits. Curves like Amelia Clark's should've been illegal.

Her hand fell on mine before she yanked the pillow into her arms and turned to the side away from me. "Thanks." She snuggled into it, accidently rubbing against me.

We both froze. My attraction to her wasn't exactly subtle in that moment. My cock was fully hard and so fucking angry for the lack of attention it had been getting all week. With temptation like her in front of it, I knew I couldn't go another night without getting myself off. Sex with Amelia was out of the question. I was so far gone, I couldn't even begin to imagine how tight her cunt would feel wrapped around my cock, draining it of an entire week's worth of buildup.

"Tobias?"

Her voice was quiet, but I heard her clearly against my pounding heart.

"Amelia," I returned. It was all my choked voice could make out from lack of oxygen. I was afraid to breathe. I was afraid to move.

"You can move closer if you want." She took in a deep breath, and I blinked a few times, wondering if I'd heard her right.

After a few seconds, I realized she wasn't going to give me any more hints about what to do, so I closed the distance, sliding my body flush against hers and resting my palm on her stomach. I could resist her, but I didn't want to. Even as my mind tried desperately to push thoughts of her away, her scent was too strong. Her presence too dominant. I needed her, and I would take whatever she would allow.

My mouth landed at the back of her neck just as she pressed her ass against me. I groaned in surprise then gently bit down on her skin in response. "Careful, Birthday Girl. You don't know what you're tempting down there."

"What if I want to find out?" Small fingers landed on mine. "Would you let me?"

My eyes pinched shut as my fingers traveled down until I found the edge of her top. Pulling up gently, I wet the spot I had bitten with my tongue. "You don't have to ask me twice."

I could feel the quickening of her belly as my fingers traveled down.

My mouth dipped again, my lips moving around the crook of her neck. She shivered in my hold, and I groaned again at the feel of my dick sliding between her ass cheeks. She felt so good in my arms—small, yet thick in all the right places.

My palm slipped down farther, making it into her panties. Her legs chose that moment to clench together, so I paused.

"No?" I asked. If she didn't want me, I wouldn't pressure her. I started to slide my hand out.

She placed her hand on mine and squeezed then pulled it back down. "Yes. Just…" I could practically hear her nervous swallow. "Go slow, okay?"

Amelia didn't have to tell me she was a virgin. I already knew, thanks to my sister's late-night overshares. But in this case, that knowledge proved beneficial.

"Are you sure? We don't have to—"

"Shut up, Tobias." Her hand found mine again, this time wrapping around it and guiding it down until my fingers found her clit.

My head fogged at the sudden heat rushing between her thighs. *Fuck.* I could almost feel the gush of sticky liquid before I'd even made her come. God, I wanted to make her come.

I let my finger play with her sensitive bud for a minute before slipping down more. Her legs opened slowly, but by the time my finger was poised above her opening and ready to sink in, they were wide and flexing farther.

With my mouth buried in her neck and my heart already racing, I found her wet opening and pushed my finger inside. I knew it wouldn't take much to get her off, especially when she started to moan and squirm in my hold.

My slow and steady pace was driving me crazy—and her too, from the feel of it. Her body moved against mine as my finger dove deeper.

I didn't know how much longer I could last without burying my cock inside her, so far I would never find my way out. But this wasn't something I wanted to rush. I wanted to savor each and every moan and the feel of her dainty but fierce nails digging into my wrist like she was encouraging me and fighting me at the same time.

Every time I opened my mouth to say anything, I stopped, too afraid that speaking my thoughts would scare her away. I couldn't exactly tell her how hot and tight her cunt was. It was so tight, my cock would have to work its way in there nice and slow.

I wondered if she had ever heard words like that before. Sure, she was a virgin, but had she ever felt thick fingers spreading her open? Something told me she hadn't.

"Just trust me, okay?" I breathed in her ear.

She nodded, and I slipped my finger from her heat and spread her juices around. When I slid back in between her lips, I added my index finger, plunging deep until her moan was so loud, it filled the tent. I quickened my pace, my fingers fluttering inside her, quickening gradually until I could feel the walls of her clench around me in warning.

"Tobias, I—" Her near-plea was cut off by a scream tearing past her throat as she came, gushing around my fingers like I'd just punctured the skin of the sweetest fruit.

My breathing was heavy from the rush of adrenaline. I'd forgotten how good it felt to explore a woman, to tease her while helping her climb to the highest peak, and getting to watch her fly then freefall without any fear of how hard she might land. It wasn't like me to fall right along with her, but I could feel my self-control unravel bit by bit as I landed right alongside her.

"Fuck." My fingers slipped from her folds as I turned onto my back. I yanked down my shorts and briefs then put a choke hold on my cock. A groan tore from my throat at the first stroke. Relief would come soon.

Amelia shifted her body so she was hovering over me, watching. Her tongue darted out, wetting her lips, as she took me in… all of me. That was hardly fair.

"Can I help?" she asked, so innocently I had to bite back my smile.

"I'm almost there." My gaze traveled to her tits, which were still fully clothed. I should have thought about that earlier. "Can I see you?"

She followed my gaze. Slowly, she peeled off her tank top, revealing her sports bra. Without even needing me to ask, she removed that too, leaving a perfect pair of breasts I'd seen once before only five days ago. I couldn't have forgotten them if I'd tried.

My eyes slipped down to her shorts. I wanted to see all of her. She lifted her hips and slid down her shorts and panties until she was completely bare and so fucking beautiful.

"Sit on me."

Her eyes were so wide and terrified of whatever came next. It was only fair. I was terrified too. If this had been a year ago or if it had been anyone else, I wouldn't even hesitate on how far to take things. But I didn't want Amelia to have regrets when it was all over. She deserved better.

She sat up, her soft body glistening from coming just moments ago. When she spread her legs to straddle me, I could see exactly what I'd done to her. She moved up my legs until she was just below my cock, giving me a perfect view of everything I never knew I wanted.

This week had opened my eyes to so much, and Amelia was the focal point.

I didn't want it to end.

And with that last thought, the buildup reached its brink. My eyes never left hers as the intensity of my climax shook me long and hard. I rode it out, catching every drop in the shirt she'd removed.

"I'm just going to need a minute," I rasped as I tried to catch my breath.

"For what?" Amelia's eyes were wide and filled with an adorable innocence.

Jesus fuck, she's beautiful. I cupped her face with my palm and pulled her lips closer to mine, brushing my nose against hers. As much as I wanted to kiss her pretty mouth, I knew I couldn't let this be her first kiss. There was a different type of intimacy that came with a first kiss, one I couldn't let be wasted because we were in the heat of it all.

No. Amelia deserved a proper first kiss, even if I had to fuck her first.

Chapter 11

AMELIA

His eyes finally fell shut after what appeared to be the most intense orgasm I'd ever witnessed. Not that I'd witnessed any other than my own. Still, I couldn't imagine it always being so thrilling, erratic, and pleasurable. Or maybe that was exactly how it was supposed to be.

His breathing was heavy and slowing while I felt a need deep in my core. I was desperate for him to continue exploring me, to feel him in all the places he wanted to touch me, to feel him in all the places I'd secretly imagined him going.

I bit my bottom lip. "Think you can do that again?" I leaned down, sliding my nose along his jaw until I reached his ear. "This time inside me?" My voice was raspy as my breath skated across his skin.

He sucked in a breath just as another quiver shook me. Tobias's grip was firm on my waist as I hovered over him, just inches from his cock. I could put him inside me and move the way I'd seen on those videos Trinity had shown me. I could toss my head back and moan as he stared at my tits bobbing before him.

But even if I wanted to make that first move, he wasn't about to let me come down on him. He just held me there, tightening and loosening his grip like he was debating something in his head.

"Do you see that first aid kit right behind me?"

I looked up and spotted the red box immediately. Nodding, I looked back down at him curiously. "Are you okay?"

He gave a wolfish grin that melted my insides. "I have condoms in there."

My pulse quickened. "Oh."

Are we actually doing this? I wanted to... with him.

I wasn't sure why I was surprised that he wanted to sleep with me too. We were on spring break, alone, with an obvious mutual attraction that had been festering for some time. Longer for me than for him, I was certain, but it was mutual for sure. And we only had two more days before we had to return to Malibu.

Besides, this was Tobias, a guy I'd contained my feelings for since before I had boobs. He was hot. He was single. And he'd already proven to be good with his hands.

"This isn't going to be weird after, right?"

He chuckled. "No, it doesn't have to be weird. It's just sex, Amelia."

To him it might've been just sex, but for me, it was more.

"But we don't have to go further if you don't want to."

I may have internally swooned. The fact that he cared about me consenting was sexy.

I swallowed then started to lower myself to answer his question. But before I could feel him, he slapped a hand to the back side of my leg to stop me. "Wait. Scoot forward first."

My heart felt like it might explode as I listened and inched my way up, still straddling him as I crawled my way toward the kit. The entire time, I felt his eyes on me—all of me.

Something warm skated across my center, and I realized it was Tobias, so close I could feel each breath hit me.

He groaned and slid his palms around the outsides of my legs until he reached my ass. I'd already forgotten the mission I was on as I felt his breath on more of me. His mouth was so close, I felt the rumble in his chest as he palmed me from behind and pulled me closer. My stomach muscles tensed. My breathing was a staccato as I waited for whatever came next.

Then I felt it. One swift swipe of his tongue found me, tasted me, and I fell forward, slamming my palms against the back of the truck. "Holy fuck," I groaned. Everything inside me clenched at the sensation.

He chuckled, the vibration of his mouth tickling me and driving me crazy. He swiped again and again, until I felt the flat of his tongue press hard against my clit. Then he sucked. Holy God, did he suck. But it wasn't until he pushed one of his thick fingers inside me that I screamed.

"I'm ready for you now," he rasped, his mouth still on me. It took a second for me to understand he was talking about the condom.

I inhaled deeply and fumbled on the latch of the first aid kit, all the while trying to ignore the gentle licks he repeated against my clit. My hand found the foil, and I passed it behind me until Tobias grabbed it and turned his focus from eating me out to situating his cock.

Moving back down his body, I watched as he slowly rolled the condom on. He sat up when he was done and flipped me onto my back like it was effortless. Then he spread my legs with his knees. My eyes grazed his shirtless body. He was a god, firm and lean, chiseled to perfection. I didn't think guys like him existed, not in real life anyway.

His hands moved over me, smoothing my skin, finding every dip and curve with his fingers, and brushing lightly over my nipples.

"You must think I'm a saint for not trying to fuck you sooner, because I wanted to, Amelia. God knows I wanted to."

I swallowed nervously. "You did?"

His eyes widened on mine, and he leaned in to brush my lips with his. "Yes. Maybe since before that day I changed your tire. But you crawled under my skin that day. I couldn't figure it out then, but I think I know now."

"You do?"

He nodded, and that was when I felt the tip of his shaft find my entrance. I gasped, but he didn't push it in. Instead, he held himself there as he moved his mouth to my ear. "You remind me of a better version of myself, a version I'd forgotten. But you're good, Amelia. And you should know, I don't do good well."

My hands found his thick, firm ass. "Don't be good for me. Not tonight." I swallowed at what I was asking. "Tonight, I need bad." I pulled him down until he took my initiative to sink in the rest of the way.

I didn't know to expect that type of pressure, like he was pulling me open from the inside, like he was working his way into something forbidden. Although I'd just granted him access, my body still wasn't ready for him. He was so big and thick as he eased himself inside me, slowly widening me beyond what I knew I was capable of, until he couldn't go any farther.

He fell into my neck and groaned. "Fuck," he cussed loudly. "You don't even realize how good you feel, do you? This is how addictions start." He moved his head up and looked me in my eyes. "Are you okay? You're quiet."

I sucked in a breath and nodded.

"I'll go slow."

Just the softness of his words lit me up inside. I wanted to feel good for him. I also wanted him to know that although this was all new for me, he made me feel good too.

He kept his promise as he moved against me. His thrusts were slow and deep, letting me get used to him. And I did. At some point, all the resistance my body had put up in the beginning released, and our movements became smoother, more rhythmic, until I was moving with him.

"Tobias," I warned once everything started quickening.

He slowed in response before pushing deeper. I spread my legs farther to accommodate more of him, until whatever spool he'd been winding inside me gave way from the spindle, unraveling at record speed. I cried out my release, shock and bliss elevating me on a natural high I never wanted to end. Maybe it didn't have to.

My eyes finally opened to find him looking at me. His movements were as slow as when he'd sent me soaring, almost delicate, like he didn't want to push me past my comfort zone. Then he was unraveling too. I could tell by the change in his movements, the hitch in his breath, and the final groan as he pushed into me one last time.

I don't know how much time passed as we lay there, waiting for our breaths to slow, with our gazes locked and our bodies still connected. But I knew I didn't want to ever forget this feeling—this desperate need to be close to another human the way I was with him, to be so intimate yet feel so safe.

My lids were already heavy. My limbs felt like noodles. And though I couldn't begin to imagine what tomorrow would bring, we would always have tonight.

Chapter 12

TOBIAS

"Hey, sis," I hissed into my phone. "One sec." I didn't need to keep quiet. Amelia was a heavy sleeper. Even when my phone notifications had started pinging like crazy after I'd turned it on, she hadn't moved a muscle.

I slid out from under the covers, stealing another look at the girl who'd kept me up all night with her curiosity. Her naked shoulder was a reminder of last night—the way we fit, the way we moved, and how neither of us could get enough.

Hopping from the bed of the truck and onto the ground, I was well aware that I was buck-ass naked as I strolled to the edge of the bluff, my phone still pressed to my ear. It was so windy, I could hear the sides of the tent flapping behind me.

"Is that a helicopter?"

"Nah, just some wind," I finally said. "How's the Big Apple?"

She sighed dramatically, which told me there must have been a change in plans that she wasn't happy with. "It's over."

"What do you mean, it's over?"

"We flew home yesterday but didn't get in until past midnight. Where the hell are you?"

"Uh…" I ran a hand through the thick nest of hair on my head, quickly debating what to tell her. I sure as hell couldn't tell her the truth. Well, not all of it anyway. "I'm on a camping trip far, far away."

I could almost hear my sister roll her eyes. "Any chance you can make it back today?"

I was genuinely confused as I thought over her question. I didn't understand why it mattered to Trinity when I came home.

"No can do, sis. We'll be back tomorrow."

"We?"

I cringed, realizing I'd said too much. And from the silence on the line, I knew my sister's rage was rising with her curiosity. "Who are you with?"

I hated how protective she could be. It had gotten worse after she'd found out about the adoption. She took inventory of everyone I spent time with and questioned my every step. All the more reason it was time for me to grow the fuck up and figure out my future.

I sighed. "Just a friend, Trin."

"I hate that you didn't come with us." Her voice was quieter now, and I couldn't stand the guilt that shot through me.

Trinity had begged me to go to New York with our parents, but I just couldn't. I couldn't pretend like nothing had changed.

It wasn't that I couldn't forgive my parents for what they'd done. Keeping my adoption from me was admittedly selfish on their part, but they were still the ones who'd raised me, taken care of me, loved me. It wasn't them who'd abandoned me.

But forgiving and forgetting were two separate things. I could never forget how terrified I'd been when I found out the truth or how that hurt had cut me so deeply, I'd given myself no other option but to run from it all, to run from myself.

For the first time since it all went down almost one year ago, I finally realized I'd only made my situation worse by escaping in the heat of the moment. It was a decision that had festered and grown to the point of— what felt like—no return.

I was in no rush to get back to all that. When I did return home, I knew things would have to be different. I couldn't hide anymore. I owed my future a chance. Plus, I wanted more time in Big Sur with Amelia, time I knew could never exist outside of the bubble we'd created. Big Sur was ours, but Malibu… it was theirs. I wouldn't let Trinity take this time from me.

"I'll see you tomorrow. Okay, Trin? I need to go." I pulled my phone from my ear to end the call, knowing the longer we stayed on the phone, the more guilt she would try to drive into me.

"Tobias," she shouted, making me cringe before I could get to the button. "You don't understand. You need to come home *today*."

My adrenaline sped with her panic. "Why? What's the rush?"

"Damn it, Tobias. Why do you have to be so difficult? It was supposed to be a surprise."

Now I was more confused than ever. It wasn't my birthday or anyone else's that I knew of. "A good surprise or a bad surprise?"

She let out a frustrated scream. "Mom and Dad met up with a sports agent in New York. His name is Aaron Wells. Ever heard of him?"

I could feel the shift in my world the moment my sister spoke that name. Did I know Aaron Wells? I may have dropped basketball from my life, but I still spoke the language. I still followed the stats and the draft. Aaron Wells, once a point guard for the Chicago Bulls, was one of the fiercest sports agents in the game. He knew how to pick 'em young and make his players money in lasting contracts.

"I've heard of him." I tried to sound nonchalant while my nerves shot off like lightning inside me.

"Well, he flew to Malibu to meet you. He knows your story and that you had a minor setback. He thinks you still have a shot at the NBA, Tobias. But he needs to know that you want this."

"I want this." The words flew from my mouth before I could even speak. "I want this, Trin. But..." I glanced over my shoulder at my truck, where Amelia still slept. My heart twisted. "I need some time. Will he wait until tomorrow?"

"No." My sister's irritation was a slap in the face. *Of course he won't wait.* "Where are you, Tobias?"

"I'm camping in Big Sur."

Silence passed over the line again. If my sister understood anything about me, it was my need for time alone. "I can contain him until tonight. But if you're serious about still wanting a shot at this, then don't mess it up over a spring fling or whatever."

I had to bite my tongue from defending Amelia. Maybe she was a spring fling, but she was also more. She was inspiration and excitement and home wrapped up in a gorgeous package. But that battle would have to be fought later.

My pulse had already quickened, but now my veins felt fiery with adrenaline. "All right, I'll head home. You better not be fucking with me, Trin."

"I wouldn't do that to you. I know how much you've missed basketball. We all know, even though you never talk about it."

There's that guilt I was trying to avoid. "I'll start packing up. Thanks for looking out, sis."

"Just get your ass home."

I hung up and walked back to the truck, slipping inside just as Amelia's eyes flickered open. Her cheeks reddened almost instantly, and a smile broke out on her face. There was no denying how beautiful she was. And the fact that I was the cause for that smile was all the more reason to smile back.

But I couldn't. Not knowing what I had to do next.

"Hey," she said, her voice chalky from little rest.

"Hey." I slipped under the covers and wrapped my arm around her naked waist. Her skin was smooth like silk and warm under the soft blankets. My hand slipped over her hips, loving the way her curves created a journey I could explore all day if I were only allowed the time.

She looked back at me with the widest gaze, her long lashes batting down as she waited for me to speak. She smiled shyly and wiggled her way closer to me then opened the blanket to cover me too. My eyes slipped to catch a quick glimpse of what I'd become so familiar with last night.

Once her body was pressed to mine, I let my gaze drift over her face while my fingers brushed the underside of her jaw. I loved this angle of her more than I should. The light from the morning sun rained down on her through the clear ceiling of the tent, making her eyes appear lighter than they already were. My six-three form hovered over all five-one of her. Her lips formed a slight pout, and that was where my gaze stuck.

"Everything okay?" Her voice was soft, but I could hear the worry it carried.

"I think so." I traced her jaw with my fingers as I spoke. "Trin called—" I paused as Amelia's eyes narrowed, and then I cringed. "I know I said no cell phones, but I just wanted to check in quickly."

Her expression relaxed. "Okay, so what did Trinity have to say?"

"There's an agent at my house who wants to meet me. He's kind of a big deal in the NBA world."

"Really?" she asked with excitement. "That's great news. You want to meet him, right?"

I nodded, still averting her gaze. "I do."

"Then what's wrong?" Her hand slipped up my chest as she spoke, blazing a fire trail with her touch.

I finally met her gaze, deciding right then and there to cut all the bullshit from my life. And that included hiding everything I felt. "What would you say if I asked you out?"

"Like—on a date?"

My cheeks heated. "Yeah, like on a date."

Her eyes flickered between mine, and her smile faded. My chest clenched with worry. "I don't know, Tobias."

Her hesitance hurt. "It's like that, huh? Damn." I started to pull away, but Amelia pulled me back, her grip like a vise on my arm.

"Stop. It's not like that."

"Then what's it like?" I frowned as I stared down at her, trying desperately not to become more frustrated than I already was. "I know last night was just sex, but I like you."

Her eyes widened slightly. "You do?"

I blew out a breath. This was not going the way I'd hoped. "Yes. I mean, I think so. Don't you like me?"

"Yes. I like you, Tobias. But Trinity made it clear how she felt about us dating."

My brows pulled together. My sister was never subtle with her feelings. I'd always known Amelia was off limits, but now I was beginning to question the reasons why. "When was this?"

"Well, we were really young, but—"

I rolled my eyes and cut her off before she could continue. "She'll get over it. We can talk to her."

Amelia didn't look very convinced. "You really think she'll get over it?"

"Why wouldn't she? We're all adults now." I believed my words with a conviction I felt everywhere.

Amelia's expression changed, like she was trying to let my words sway her. "Maybe you're right."

"Of course I'm right." I smiled, leaning down until my nose touched hers. I felt her shake in my arms, and I knew without a shadow of a doubt we were making the right decision. "You know what else I'm right about?"

"What?" Her voice was breathy, and her eyes began to close.

"You're a good kisser."

She laughed as her lids opened again to meet my eyes. "How would you know? You've never even kissed me."

I brushed my lips against hers. "But I'm about to."

Without delay, I pressed my lips to hers and felt her melt right along with me. My head spun as she moaned into my mouth and gripped me harder. Her dainty fingers dug into my arm like she needed the leverage to hold on to. I moved my hand from her jaw to her waist, pulling her against me as I parted her lips with mine.

Everything was warm—my head, my chest, her breath, my cock. Fuck, we needed to leave. I pulled away, determined to make the date with her happen as soon as humanly possible.

Our breaths were heavy as I placed another kiss on her cheek. "You ready to go home?"

"No. But I'll help you pack." She smiled and pulled off the covers before searching for her clothes.

Damn. She was beautiful. No. She was more than beautiful. Amelia Clark was a goddess.

I wrapped my arm around her waist and pulled her beneath me, watching as her dark-brown hair fanned around her head. "On second thought," I said as I placed her arms above her head and widened her legs with my knees, "The NBA can wait. One more for the road?"

She giggled as I dipped down for another kiss, simultaneously reaching between her legs and teasing her clit with my thumb. Her giggle quickly turned into a moan as her back arched and her hips pushed up into my hand.

"Only if you promise to buy me dinner," she finally said.

I grinned. "That's a deal." I captured her hard nipple in my mouth before swirling my tongue around its peak.

Whoever had said spring flings couldn't last was wrong.

Amelia and I were about to prove it.

I hope you enjoyed *Falling from Gravity*. Want more? You can check out Amelia and Tobias's full-length story in *Defying Gravity* now!

SMARTURL.IT/DEFYINGGRAVITY_NOVEL

Turn the page to keep reading more about Amelia and Tobias in the prologue and the first chapter of *Defying Gravity*.

Prologue

AMELIA

Somewhere between my childhood home and the long stretch of Malibu Beach that I had once called my backyard, a familiar figure came into view.

His long lashes flickered down as he blew out a breath. His wide eyes narrowed in the direction of the bare feet he'd shoved deep into the sand. Early age lines wrinkled his tan forehead, and a scowl rested on his face.

My heart jolted in my chest as unease churned in my gut. Three years later and the sight of Tobias James could still knock me off my axis.

He was a few feet away when he looked up and spotted me. The moment was lightning, illuminating his surprise. His lids widened, revealing a circular sea, endless in its depth, and for a vulnerable instant, I thought I might have left my anchor there.

Once upon a time, I looked into those same eyes and saw my past, my present, and my future. I was certain every sacred dream would come to fruition when the time was right—but we were young ... and life had other plans for us.

Chapter 1

AMELIA

PART ONE - THREE YEARS EARLIER

A rattling sound shook me awake and jolted my gaze toward my bedroom window. It was black outside, save for a few twinkling stars and the moon's glow. I shook my head, hoping to clear the fog from a deep sleep.

It was a miracle I'd been able to doze off with the blare of the music and boisterous voices coming from upstairs. My parents were party animals. It wasn't unusual for them to throw some random shindig in the middle of the week to celebrate any small accomplishment that came through their firm. Clients—mostly actors, producers, and casting agents—were their everything, their bread and butter. No one cared that the teenager downstairs had school in the morning.

My eyes adjusted to the clock on my nightstand—3:25 a.m. I blinked again, noticing that the loud bass from the stereo system's surround sound was nonexistent now. The party was apparently over, but the rattling sounded again, followed by a tap-tap-tapping against glass.

I jerked my head toward the French doors that led to the back patio. My eyes landed on the figure begging for entry at my door. Tall, hooded, wide crystal blues pointed straight at me. Flutters ignited under my ribs.

Snatching my silk sheet from my bed, I pulled it to my chest on instinct, awakening completely and sitting up moments after recognizing him.

Tobias.

I jumped up and ran toward him, a smile blossoming on my face. I couldn't help it. It had been five days since our secret spring break trip to Big Sur, where we camped out in his pickup truck, just the two of us. And every day since we'd been back, he would sneak into my room, and we would pick up where we'd left off up on that mountain, thinking no one would ever be the wiser.

After turning the lock and then the knob, I tugged on the handle, and he stepped into my room, filling the space as he always did, with confidence and intention.

"You're late," I accused as he pulled me into his hulky arms. He was so tall, my head rested on the lower half of his chest as his build practically swallowed me. I sighed into him, breathing in his freshly showered scent of cedar wood and coconut.

"I was waiting for things to die down," he said. "I sent you a text telling you I didn't want to risk being seen."

I looked toward my bed, where my phone lay, and it dawned on me. *Crap. I never put it on the charger.* "It must have died after I fell asleep." I gave him my exaggerated pout. "It's too late to watch a movie now."

He chuckled and leaned down, his lips skimming my nose. "We never watch much of the movie, anyway."

He was right. I could never concentrate on a movie when I was busy guessing the journey his mouth and hands would take as we lay together. Narrowing my eyes, I pulled him toward my bed. "But pretending is so much fun."

His mouth curled with obvious amusement. "You sure about that?"

Refusing to answer, I lay down, letting my brown hair fan around me as Tobias followed. He faced me, lowering himself until he was hovering dangerously close.

In the past week, I'd gotten used to this routine. To us. But Tobias was never supposed to crawl under my skin. We were only supposed to be a spring fling.

I stroked his cheek, memorizing every strong line of his face and loving the smooth texture of his skin as he kissed my palm. His lids closed at my touch.

Turning my head, I let my eyes flicker to the moon outside the double doors. I pulled in a deep breath. The exhale was cleansing, and for a moment, I forgot that the countdown to our end was ticking in the distance.

When I was with him, I didn't want to think about him leaving for basketball and me leaving for dance. I wanted to spend every minute making up for lost time. Tobias and I had known each other since we were kids; he was my neighbor as well as my best friend's older brother. But I never *really* knew him, not the way I wanted to know him now.

"What would you have studied if you didn't have basketball?"

He appeared to ponder that for a moment before propping up on his elbow. When he spoke, he ran his finger along the edge of my waistband. "That's easy. Sports management. I don't know if I ever saw a life for myself without basketball in it. But even thinking about my future—once I retire from the NBA—I'd love to teach or coach." His eyes flickered to mine. "What about you? What would you want to study if you didn't have your sights set on being an NBA dancer?"

"Something in physics, I think."

He pulled back, an amused gleam in his eyes. "Really?"

Shrugging, I pointed at my window, where the moon hung perfectly in the frame. "I've always been fascinated with nature and the mechanics behind it all. My parents got sick of me always asking 'how' and handed me a set of encyclopedias." I laughed, knowing how that sounded. "Yeah, almanacs. For extremely liberal parents whose careers relied on communication media, they had a thing against overstimulation before the age of thirteen. Whenever I had a question, I'd pull those suckers out and go down the rabbit hole of theories."

"Theories, huh?" He bent his head, bringing his nose to my neck, running it along my sensitive skin before placing a gentle kiss there. "What's your favorite one?"

I smiled. "The misconception of the moon's strength. The moon may be small, but it's powerful enough to move oceans."

He shifted so he was looking into my eyes. "Really?"

Nodding, I ran my fingers up his arm, hating that nagging reminder in the back of my mind that one of these nights would be our last. "How do you think the ocean tides are formed?"

He pitched a brow. "From the moon?"

"Close. From earth's gravitational attraction of the moon. Anyway, I think it's kind of magical how powerful the moon's pull is. How a black piece of rock in the sky can move oceans, light up the midnight sky, and stabilize the rotation of the largest terrestrial planet in our solar system."

A strand of hair fell into his eye during my geek out. I was moving it away when his lip tipped at the corner. "Did you just use the term 'terrestrial planet'?"

I pushed against him with a laugh. "Yes, kinda like you use the words 'drive penetration,' 'pin downs,' and 'shooting fundamentals.'" I cringed at my choice of terms as Tobias threw his head back and laughed.

Growling, I pushed him onto his back and moved to sit up. He caught himself on his elbows, shot his arms out for me, and pulled me onto his lap. His chin tipped up. Mine tipped down. And our lust-infused smiles met.

"How does it feel to be the short one?" I teased.

His hands were lightly skimming the tops of my thighs. "Feels damn good." He continued his ascent until his palms were cupping my ass through my yoga pants. "Glad you asked."

Laughing, I leaned down, teasing his lips with mine. "You know what else feels good?"

His blue eyes darkened. "Oh, I have an idea."

Gentle fingers plucked at the hint of pink fabric peeking out from my pants. Pinching back a smile, I wiggled above him.

His nose flared as he growled and pulled me closer. With my knees wrapped around him and my chest pressed to his, he buried his next words in my neck. "You tease me like you don't think I'd rip these clothes right off you."

My entire body heated as I tripped on my next breath. "You threaten me like that would be a bad thing."

The corner of his mouth curled with what I hoped was wicked intention. "You're sassy when I interrupt your sleep. I think I like it a little too much."

"I think you like *me* a little too much."

He shrugged, his eyes slipping from mine and moving down my neck. "You might be right. Doesn't change anything, though, does it? We decided to keep things between us a secret."

Detecting something new in his tone, I pulled back to look at him. "We did. And it was the right thing to do."

His brows crinkled, and I couldn't help wondering if he was having second thoughts. But why? We'd talked about "what came next" a dozen times after coming home. It was a mutual decision to keep things between us on the downlow.

Eventually, he nodded. "Yeah, Trin would be pissed."

That was an understatement, and we both knew it. Trinity, Tobias's younger sister and my best friend, had always been protective of her older brother. She had threatened me years ago, telling me I was dead to her if I so much as flirted with her brother. I'd spent years honoring her wishes until not a single wish on earth could have saved me from falling for the boy next door.

At times, I thought she couldn't possibly feel the same way that she had when we were thirteen. We were old enough to freely choose who we wanted to get involved with.

But I saw the way Trinity guarded Tobias like he was a forbidden Egyptian tomb. And how she talked about him like he was a troubled Lost

Boy whom only she could ever understand. This past year, especially, had been the worse. It wasn't until Tobias filled me in on the big family secret during our spontaneous spring break trip that I began to understand the change in my best friend.

Tobias had been adopted as a baby, and their parents hid it from everyone, including their children. When he'd stumbled upon his adoption papers last year, it changed the path of everything Tobias had been working for since he was a kid. His dreams of getting drafted shattered in the blink of an eye. He couldn't focus on school, basketball, or anything besides the lie he told himself—that he no longer belonged. He referred to it as his spiral.

Once I learned all that, Trinity's slow turn in behavior started to make sense. She'd gone from protective to possessive. Like she had something to prove now that they weren't blood related.

"It's more than Trinity's ego I'm worried about," I said with a sad smile. "We can't get all wrapped up in feelings. It would be so easy to—" I forced out a sigh.

His eyes pleaded with mine. "What were you going to say?"

"Nothing." I shook my head, knowing I had to tread carefully. Any talk of feelings would be dangerous territory. "You're entering the draft. You'll end up moving to who knows where, and—"

"Back up, Amelia. Hopefully, I'm *draft eligible*, which doesn't guarantee me a job. I sent in my letter a few days ago, and I won't be getting any kind of response for a few weeks. With my history, dropping out of college ball before the championship, they probably won't even consider me for the combine, which makes my chances shoddy at best."

"Combine?"

"It's like a showcase where teams measure the skills of top-level prospects. Only a select bunch make it through."

My jaw dropped. "But you have that agent now. He knows the scouts. He helped you explain why you had to drop when you did. And you still have your stats from when you did play. You'll get in. You're meant to play ball. Aaron Wells came to you for a reason. So, *when you do* get invited to the combine, who knows where you'll end up after the draft. And I'll be in LA."

His brows pulled together. "It sounds like you've been giving this some thought."

"Haven't you?"

He didn't even hesitate to nod. "Yeah, actually. I have. I meant what I said in Big Sur. I want to take you out on a real date. Dinner. Movies. The beach. We don't have long before one of us leaves, and honestly—" He swallowed. "The more time we spend together, the more I want to tell Trin."

Panic clutched my chest, breaking my heart in the process. "We can't."

"Why not? I could get picked up by the Lions. Then I'd be in LA, too."

I sighed heavily. "And if you don't? What if we tell Trinity about us and she hates us for it? It will ruin whatever time we have left. And is hurting Trin really worth it if you do leave?" Maybe it was selfish of me, but I didn't want Tobias to have to choose between his sister and me. I worried it would come down to that.

His eyes moved between mine as his jaw tightened. "I see you've got this all figured out already. Thanks for consulting me."

I cupped his face in my hands. "Stop. I don't want us to do anything we might regret later. Being together feels right, but once you're gone—"

"I only play ball five months out of the year."

"Yeah, and then there's preseason and off-season practice, training, promo. You think you'll have time for me? You think you'll even remember me?"

"Amelia—"

I shook my head, cutting him off and swallowing my emotion. I refused to let either of us dwell on the what-ifs. "Let's just wait a few more weeks. The draft is in June, right? You'll know where you're going at that point."

He stared at me for what felt like forever, his eyes swimming with so many words I wanted to probe out of him, but I knew there would be no turning back after hearing them. Things were so new between us, I didn't want either of us regretting a single decision. And giving us time to make those decisions felt right.

I gave him a small smile in an attempt to lighten the mood. "Just think. We could both be joining the NBA in a few months."

Tobias didn't smile, which made my insides stir, but he started to nod slowly. That slight acknowledgment was enough to give me my next breath. Then his eyes dimmed as he tilted his face up, pointing his mouth toward mine.

I leaned in, brushing my lips against his, desperately wanting him to respond with the eagerness he had walked in with.

A happily ever after wasn't in the cards for us anytime soon, but for now, he was mine, and I was his. And every stolen moment was one I would attempt to stretch for as long as possible.

Want more? Read *Defying Gravity* here:

SMARTURL.IT/DEFYINGGRAVITY_NOVEL

MORE BOOKS BY
K.K. ALLEN

CONTEMPORARY ROMANCE

Center of Gravity

Falling From Gravity (Short Story)

Defying Gravity

ROMANTIC SUSPENSE

Waterfall Effect

NEW ADULT ROMANCE

Up in the Treehouse

Under the Bleachers

Through The Lens (Release TBD)

ROCK STAR ROMANCE

Dangerous Hearts

Destined Hearts

YOUNG ADULT FANTASY

Summer Solstice Enchanted

The Equinox

The Descendants

CONNECT WITH
K.K. ALLEN

Mailing List: www.smarturl.it/KK_MailList

Website & Blog: www.kkallen.com

Facebook: www.facebook.com/AuthorKKAllen

Goodreads: www.goodreads.com/KKAllen

BookBub: www.bookbub.com/profile/k-k-allen

Instagram: www.instagram.com/kkallen_author

Twitter: www.twitter/KKAllenAuthor

JOIN K.K.'S INSIDERS GROUP, FOREVER YOUNG!

Enjoy special sneak peeks, participate in exclusive giveaways,

enter to win ARCs, and chat it up with K.K. and special guests ;)

www.facebook.com/groups/foreveryoungwithkk

About the Author

K.K. Allen is an award-winning USA Today Bestselling author who writes heartfelt and inspirational contemporary romance stories mainly about "capturing the edge of innocence." K.K. graduated with a degree in interdisciplinary arts and sciences from the University of Washington and currently works as a digital producer for a leading online educational institution. She resides in central Florida, and is the mother to a ridiculously handsome little dude who owns her heart.

K.K.'s publishing journey began in June 2014 with the YA Contemporary Fantasy trilogy, The Summer Solstice. In 2016, K.K. published her first Contemporary Romance, Up in the Treehouse, which went on to win the Romantic Times 2016 Reviewers' Choice Award for Best New Adult Book of the Year. With K.K.'s love for inspirational and coming-of-age stories involving heartfelt narratives and honest emotions, you can be assured to always be surprised by what K.K. releases next.

Stay tuned for more information about upcoming projects by connecting with K.K. in all the social media spaces.

WWW.KKALLEN.COM